**"Are you kidnapping me?" she asked coolly, folding her arms over her chest.**

"I could, I suppose, but no. I'm going, Betty. You can either get in and come with me and help, or you can go back to your group. But you're not going to stop me."

Betty knew she should go back to Shay. Shay and Mallory would catch up with Garret in no time. They'd help him no matter what fuss he put up, and hopefully get him out of the fray so he could *heal*.

But he was...holding on by a thread. He needed someone to be the voice of reason. And it looked like for today it was going to have to be her.

She climbed into the passenger seat, somewhat rewarded by the fact he seemed shocked she'd agreed to go with him. But he got over his surprise quickly, skirted the front of his truck and climbed into the driver's seat.

"So, where are we going, then?" she asked.

# DODGING BULLETS IN BLUE VALLEY

---

## NICOLE HELM

⟨H⟩HARLEQUIN
INTRIGUE

For Whitney, Nick and the infamous lovey killer.

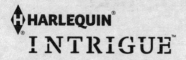

**HARLEQUIN®**
**INTRIGUE™**

PLEASE RECYCLE

Recycling programs
for this product may
not exist in your area.

ISBN-13: 978-1-335-48957-9

Dodging Bullets in Blue Valley

Copyright © 2022 by Nicole Helm

For questions and comments about the quality of this book,
please contact us at CustomerService@Harlequin.com.

Harlequin Enterprises ULC
22 Adelaide St. West, 41st Floor
Toronto, Ontario M5H 4E3, Canada
www.Harlequin.com

**Printed in U.S.A.**

**Nicole Helm** grew up with her nose in a book and the dream of one day becoming a writer. Luckily, after a few failed career choices, she gets to follow that dream—writing down-to-earth contemporary romance and romantic suspense. From farmers to cowboys, Midwest to *the* West, Nicole writes stories about people finding themselves and finding love in the process. She lives in Missouri with her husband and two sons and dreams of someday owning a barn.

### Books by Nicole Helm

### Harlequin Intrigue

### *A North Star Novel Series*

*Summer Stalker*
*Shot Through the Heart*
*Mountainside Murder*
*Cowboy in the Crosshairs*
*Dodging Bullets in Blue Valley*

### *A Badlands Cops Novel*

*South Dakota Showdown*
*Covert Complication*
*Backcountry Escape*
*Isolated Threat*
*Badlands Beware*
*Close Range Christmas*

### *Carsons & Delaneys: Battle Tested*

*Wyoming Cowboy Marine*
*Wyoming Cowboy Sniper*
*Wyoming Cowboy Ranger*
*Wyoming Cowboy Bodyguard*

Visit the Author Profile page at Harlequin.com.

# CAST OF CHARACTERS

*Garret Averly*—A sheriff in Blue Valley, Montana. Just found out about the existence of his five-month-old twins and wants to find and bring them home.

*Betty Wagner*—Doctor for North Star. Has been taking care of Garret while he heals from a gunshot wound and agrees to help him find and bring his twins home.

*Elsie Rogers*—Head of technology for North Star, now living permanently in Blue Valley with Nate Averly.

*Nate Averly*—Garret's brother. Resident of Blue Valley. Rancher.

*Savannah*—Garret's dead ex-wife, who kept his twins a secret from him.

*Shay*—Head of North Star. Good friends with Betty as they've both been around North Star from the beginning.

## Chapter One

Garret Averly was *not* used to being in constant pain. He was *definitely not* used to being incapable of doing everything for himself.

Most of all, he was not used to having a woman in his house who wasn't his ex-wife.

His *dead* ex-wife, apparently.

The past few weeks had done quite a number on him. First, he'd had to come to grips with the fact that his brother, who'd presumably come back from war paranoid and delusional two years ago, had actually been telling the truth about the military corruption he'd stumbled upon.

Not only that, some secret group had been sent to Blue Valley, Montana—of all places—to help get to the bottom of it. Keep Nate safe and prove he was telling the truth.

Then, as if that wasn't enough, said group had found out that Garret's ex-wife had been part of it, sent here to keep an eye on Nate through Garret. Bad enough to be taken in by a woman he'd thought he'd been in love with, but things had become a hundred times worse. The group had informed him Savannah had given birth to twins four months after she'd left him high and dry, and then died in childbirth.

She hadn't listed him as father to the twins, or even informed him of their existence. Instead, his ex had decided to secrete the kids off to her grandparents. The grandfather being the man who'd been black-market selling army weapons, and was indirectly responsible for Garret getting shot.

Despite being a cop, Garret had never actually been shot before. Threatened, shot at, but never actually *shot*.

He would not recommend it.

Now, he was out of commission for *weeks*, instead of doing his usual job as sheriff of Blue Valley. Stuck in his house with his dog, Barney.

And there was this…*doctor* all up in his space. While he struggled with the pain of a gunshot wound and the insurmountable information that he was a father.

To twins. Twins he'd never seen, never held, even now.

Garret appreciated that the secret group his brother had gotten himself mixed up in had helped Nate prove that he wasn't losing his mind. He was downright grateful Nate had found himself a new beginning with Elsie Rogers, said group's computer genius and former resident of Blue Valley. He was beyond indebted to them for discovering the existence of his own children, for this doctor stitching him up and performing a blood transfusion after he'd been shot.

But her still being here weeks later was starting to feel…awkward. Or perhaps worse than awkward. Comfortable. Enjoyable. She was doing her job and he was…

Well, it didn't bear thinking about. Which was why,

despite the fact he'd been up for about an hour, he hadn't left his bedroom. He'd done his rehabilitation exercises, stared out the window and grappled with too many emotions to name.

But he did not brave the world outside his bedroom walls. That world would invade soon enough.

As if on cue, there was a knock at his bedroom door and he grunted, "Come in." He knew that if he didn't answer or told her to go away, she'd just march right in and poke and prod at him until she was satisfied, so there was no point doing anything else.

"Good morning," Betty said cheerfully. She had her bag of torture devices—at least that was Garret's opinion of them—and Barney followed her into the room like he was her shadow.

Garret glared at his dog, the traitor, who now trailed Betty wherever she went, looking lovelorn and besotted, if a dog could be either.

Apparently his dog could. Garret really didn't like the fact it seemed to be rubbing off on him.

"I can walk to the kitchen. I don't need to lie in this bed," he said before she could start unpacking her supplies.

She studied him in that cool, doctor way of hers. She was petite. Couldn't be much more than five feet tall, but she managed to give off an aura of authority. Her straight black hair was always pulled back in a tidy braid, her dark eyes always cool and assessing. He didn't know how she'd gotten mixed up in this secret group of hers, but then again, he still didn't know how his brother or Elsie Rogers had, either.

Everything in his life felt like a mystery, or a confusing nightmare, at the moment. Except for maybe the throbbing pain in his shoulder. *That* he understood. He might be irritated with the constant annoyance of it, but at least that wound made sense.

"Of course you can," she said briskly and unaffectedly. "Is that what you would prefer?"

Of *course* it was what he'd prefer. Having a pretty woman touch him in his bed, no matter how efficiently and with the intent of only changing his bandage, was not exactly enjoyable. And he wasn't talking about the pain in his shoulder. "Yes."

"All right." She turned around and headed for the kitchen, giving no evidence of how she felt about the change in venue. Barney trotted right after her.

"Figures," Garret muttered.

Garret scratched his hands through his hair and then got to his feet. She always left the faint hint of vanilla wafting about behind her. He couldn't articulate why that irritated him, but it felt like an invasion of his space when this woman was quite literally keeping him from *dying*.

But he was grumpy and tired. And if he concentrated on all those bad feelings, he could mostly ignore the twisting in his stomach that hadn't dissipated since he'd found out he was a father.

A father. To twins. He'd never met.

Yeah, he'd rather get his bandage changed and focus on that pain than this one. He moved into the kitchen and sat down. Betty was methodically spreading out her supplies to change his bandage.

Garret didn't know much about her. Her name was Betty, or at least that's what she went by. Who knew if the members in this secret group used real names. She was a doctor, allegedly. Hard to doubt when she'd saved his life.

He figured somewhere she had a full dossier on him, while he knew next to nothing about her. Not even her last name. If he'd had more energy, he might have demanded to know a few more things. If he wasn't so preoccupied with the idea of his *children* out there, all this might have really bothered him.

But he couldn't get beyond the dogged exhaustion, the throbbing pain and the emotional upheaval of finding out he was a father.

For four or five months, his children had been in the world and he hadn't known. They'd been born premature and he hadn't been there to watch after them, hope and pray and worry for them.

Savannah had been dead.

A boy and a girl. His. And he'd never even laid eyes on them.

He wanted to scrub his hands over his face, but he had to keep still while Betty peeled the old bandage away and began to clean the wound. After a long silence, she spoke in her quiet, gentle way.

"You can't do this all on your own quite yet. But if you need some space, I can stay somewhere else." She said it so equitably, it took him a few moments to understand what she was saying.

Translation: stop being a grumpy jerk and taking out your frustrations on the doctor who is only doing her job, and quit acting like she's the problem.

"Where? No hotels. You don't know anybody else here besides Elsie." *So effusive and kind, Garret. Really.*

Betty's face remained impassive, but her eyes were amused. "I have my ways."

"You're fine here," he mumbled. "For the time being." He kept looking ahead at the wall while she changed his bandage. Better than studying her face like he had the first few times she'd gone through this process. High cheekbones, dark, intelligent eyes, a golden glow to her skin that was all too distracting.

But her full, sexy mouth was the real problem. Her eyes were always cool and direct when she examined his wound or changed his bandage, but her mouth was plump and sultry, and he couldn't help but want a taste. She pursed her lips, chewed on the bottom one, twisted it into all sorts of distracting shapes while she worked on him.

Yeah, best to stare at the wall.

A knock sounded on the door, but Betty didn't hurry through what she was doing. She meticulously finished the bandaging.

Once she was finished, she let Garret stand and open the door.

Elsie stood there, Nate behind her. Nate had been taking care of Garret's horses since Garret had been shot.

Though Garret's full-time job was being sheriff to Blue Valley, he kept two horses on his property and helped his father on the family ranch when he could.

Now he was ducking his parents in order to keep them from being worried, dodging his dispatch secretary, Mrs. Linley, to avoid from being clucked over and having to explain to the whole dang county how he'd been shot.

The only people who knew what had happened to him were standing right here. His brother often stopped by after feeding the horses, but not usually with Elsie. "Let me guess. You're not here for a friendly visit."

"One of these days I'll try to be," Elsie said with a smile, "but not today. Still, I've got some great news."

Garret moved out of the doorway so Nate and Elsie could enter. He eyed his brother, but Nate's face gave nothing away.

"We've finally made some headway with Mrs. Loren." Garret tried not to scowl at the name of Savannah's grandmother, who allegedly had *his* children.

"There will still be a lot of legal hoops to jump through. Especially since Mrs. Loren lives in Virginia and you live here. She hasn't agreed to give up custody or anything like that, but she's agreed to come here with the twins. So you can meet them at the very least. I know it's not what you were hoping for, but it's a big step forward."

Here. *Here.* "When?" Garret asked, holding himself too still, too tight. He would crack apart if he didn't learn to bend.

"We're coordinating to get them here as soon as possible."

BETTY WAGNER HAD worked on a lot of big, grumpy men in her time as North Star's head doctor. She'd had to crawl on top of thrashing military men, immobilize cursing, bleeding villains, and operate on, sew up and otherwise "fix" all manner of people in some of the worst situations.

But she was always in a more…controlled environment. Her old medical center, North Star headquarters, or even the field—mountains, forests, the vast Dakota Badlands. She'd done it all and seen it all.

Except stay in a man's *house* and take care of him while his adorable dog followed her around...

Like the man's eyes.

Betty had come too far to feel threatened by that, and if she'd had any qualms about staying in Garret's space, she would have voiced them. She wasn't a martyr, and she was hardly afraid of her boss, who was really more like one of her closest friends.

She didn't think Garret Averly was dangerous. But her reaction to him was *not* comfortable.

Especially when the topic was his children. Garret was so wounded over this betrayal, this loss, and it made her want to, well, fix it for him. She was a doctor. She was used to being able to sew up and heal hurts.

But these weren't those kind.

Elsie was giving the details, and Garret still stood. He didn't look pained, but he held himself too rigidly, kept his face devoid of emotion. His brother like a shadow right behind him.

Two impressively tall, broad men who'd clearly learned to hide their emotions, school their reactions and be strong in the face of threats and pain.

It really shouldn't feel any different than her years at North Star at all. She was used to exactly this.

"The most important thing is proving paternity," Elsie was saying. "She wants to use her doctor. We want to use ours."

"Why not both, then?" Betty suggested. "That way both parties can be assured of their test results."

"You can do a test?" Elsie asked.

"I can do the test, and I have a contact who can, privately, without anyone finding out, examine the results." Betty looked from Elsie to Garret. "When they land, I'll be with you. I'll give the children a full checkup myself—I can get a basic idea of health even if the grandmother doesn't let me give a full examination. We'll perform our own paternity test—no matter what the grandmother wants to do. We will make sure everything is on the up-and-up, and those kids are healthy."

"And from there, we'll help you work out the legalities of guardianship," Elsie continued.

"But…why?" Garret asked, and finally his expression betrayed at least some of the things he was feeling. Confusion chief among them.

"You were shot during one of our missions," Elsie said. "If a civilian is caught in the cross fire of things we instigated, we make sure to take care of them."

Garret nodded at his brother. "Nate instigated your case. And I'm a *sheriff*, hardly a civilian."

"Depends on how you look at it," Elsie returned. "But we're helping you out, Garret. Civilian or sheriff or brother. Consider it payment for your contribution to our mission."

"I did it for Nate," Garret said gruffly.

"Regardless," Betty said, adopting the physician voice she used when she wasn't about to argue with someone over a trivial issue. "Consider us your team to get your kids back. We don't disappear until the job is done." North Star never backed away from a challenge, and Betty in particular wasn't going to back away from an opportunity to help a father be united with his children.

Nate put his hand on Garret's good shoulder and gave it a squeeze. "Betty's right. We're your team. We'll get those kids."

Garret nodded, and Betty knew she should speak up, but she couldn't bring herself to ruin the moment.

Because, God knew, getting those kids united with their father was absolutely her end goal, but it was also clear Garret hadn't considered anything about what it would mean for him. How he would take care of them. How his life would change. Especially if he got them before he was fully healed.

Which just meant she had the time between now and when those twins came home to their father to prepare him.

# Chapter Two

Garret woke up in the middle of the night, a throbbing pain in his shoulder, a disturbing dream melting away so quickly he didn't really remember what had happened in it, just that it had been…wrong. And that wrongness lingered so much, returning to sleep wasn't possible.

Lying in bed staring at the ceiling wasn't possible, either. He was antsy, edgy—whatever darkness had been part of that dream seemed to lie over him like a weight.

He got out of bed. He'd walk around a little bit, get a drink of water, maybe go outside. Walk out to the horses. He didn't know if Betty would sleep through all that, especially if Barney could tear himself from her side and follow him, but Garret needed to move. Fresh air.

Something aside from pain and this room.

He stepped out into the hall and frowned at the faint light. When he walked into the living room, he could hear Betty's voice.

He walked into the kitchen, and she was sitting at the table in front of a computer screen—the only light on. She was talking to someone on the screen in low, even tones, clearly trying to be quiet enough not to wake him. Barney snored at her feet.

"Work on that. Call me in ten if it doesn't work," she said before closing the laptop. She turned to face him.

He cleared his throat. "Sorry, I didn't know you were up. You didn't have to end your phone call on my account."

"Oh, I didn't. I was just consulting."

Garret raised an eyebrow and looked at the clock on his stove. "Consulting with who at three in the morning?"

Betty stood and moved through the dark room with unerring accuracy. The light flipped on and Garret winced.

"Believe it or not, doctors don't have set hours. Kind of like cops."

"Especially when you work for secret groups, huh?"

She gave him a cool look that gave away nothing. "I suppose."

"You guys are pretty tight-lipped about what you do. Who you are."

"Are we?"

"I don't even know your last name."

"Do you need to?"

"Normal people don't answer questions with other questions."

"Don't know a lot of doctors, do you?"

He chuckled. Couldn't help himself. No, he didn't know a lot of doctors, or even a lot of secret-group members, but he had a feeling Betty was unique regardless. It was something about how calm she always was. It wasn't just cool under pressure, or easygoing. There was something else…something he couldn't describe because he'd never seen it in someone before.

She didn't offer her last name or any excuses. She simply stood there, as if waiting for him to say something.

Barney let out a snuffling sound and flopped over onto his other side. He opened one bleary eye and looked adoringly up at Betty.

"I don't know what he's going to do when you leave."

"He'll manage." She leaned down and scratched Barney behind the ears. "But maybe I'll steal him away from you. You'd like that, wouldn't you, sweetie?"

"Seems like you already have," Garret managed to say, though he found his voice sounding a little gruffer than he'd intended it to.

She studied him for a moment, then turned and reached up above the stove. She pulled down a bottle of acetaminophen and handed him two.

"That obvious, huh?"

"It's a long, tough healing process, Garret. Give yourself a break."

He studied the pills in his hand. "That is not my strong suit."

She chuckled, crossing to the cabinet and grabbing a glass, which she filled with water and handed him. "First step, stop dry swallowing pills."

"Efficient," he replied, though he took a sip of the water.

"Foolish," Betty replied primly. "Take care of your body and it'll take care of you."

Garret only grunted, but he drank the rest of the water she'd given him before putting the glass back down into the sink.

"I think Elsie wanted to tell you this herself, but it

might help you sleep," Betty said. "Mrs. Loren chartered a plane. They'll be here tomorrow afternoon."

It didn't hit him like a blow. Maybe he was too tired or in too much pain. It just didn't feel real at all. "Tomorrow."

"Are you ready for it?"

"Do you ever sleep?" he asked, deciding to take a tactic out of her book and answer a question with another question. Was he ready? Not in the least. How did someone meet their own children? Children who'd been hidden from him.

He'd always figured he'd have kids—in some nebulous future where he was older, more settled, and his wife hadn't walked out on him. When he was that magical "ready." But the reality of these kids was he had to figure it out—ready or not.

"I'm very lucky that I need very little sleep," Betty was saying. "I cannot say the same for you. Now, I know what you're going to say, but I could give you something that would help you sleep."

"No."

She sighed. "I figured as much. Still, the acetaminophen might help. Try to get some sleep, Garret. Your wound needs rest to heal and tomorrow will be a big day."

"A big day," he repeated. Then he shook his head. "I don't think sleep is going to help that."

Betty considered him, and it felt a bit like those dark eyes could cut right through him. Use some sort of doctor X-ray vision to see everything going on in his head.

"Remember when you said you weren't very good at cutting yourself a break?" she asked.

"Five seconds ago? Yeah, I remember."

"You're going to need to figure it out. For those kids. They don't need you to be perfect or ready. They need a father. Not a god. Not an automaton. A father."

"I wish I knew what that meant. To just…be a father. I mean, I had a good one, but…"

"Start there. You had a good example, but you won't be able to walk the same steps your father did. Let yourself figure it out. You might always know you didn't get those first few months with them, but they won't. They won't remember a thing. You're not too late. You've got time to make this work. To be what they'll need you to be."

He hadn't known what he was feeling, so it was hard to explain how she knew exactly what to say to unlock the tightness in his chest. He was still anxious over what had happened, what would, but Betty's words eased… something inside of all that worry.

Because they did, he could finally say something he'd owed her for quite a few days now. "Thanks, Betty."

BETTY COULDN'T FIGURE out why she was nervous. Maybe it was Garret's incessant pacing as they stood outside the small, private airport Mrs. Loren was scheduled to fly into.

Maybe it was that Shay was here, too, with Mallory. Elsie and Nate made sense. Nate was Garret's brother, and Elsie was Nate's girlfriend.

But Shay was the boss at North Star and Mallory was a field operative. It felt…strange for a routine meet and greet. She didn't like the way Shay and Mallory studied the sky, exchanged glances, and hadn't really explained why they'd come when North Star headquarters was in Wyoming and two North Star people were here in Montana handling things already.

Betty was used to being on the outside looking in, so to speak. She wasn't a North Star field operative. She didn't get involved in missions. She was the doctor. The one who patched people up *after* their missions. Sometimes she was on-site, but only ever to be doctor. Her job had always been to take care of the physical and sometimes emotional needs of the North Star team. She often arrived, no questions asked, did what was expected of her, and left without knowing the details.

She'd always been okay with that. Missions didn't interest her. Healing did.

But today, feeling like an outsider with what was going on made her uncomfortable. Maybe it was because she knew Garret was on the outside of this, too. In the moment, she and Garret were like pawns.

But this was Garret's life. Not a mission. His children.

"What's going on?" Betty murmured when Garret took one of his long marches away.

Shay gave her a sideways glance. "Not sure."

"But you have a theory."

Shay raised an eyebrow. "You don't usually care about my theories unless medicine is involved."

Betty knew she could play this careful and close to the vest, but her gaze traveled to Garret's pacing form.

Shay pinched the bridge of her nose. "I swear to God, if you fall for this guy and I lose you, too…"

It wasn't falling…exactly. Betty was involved. Deeper than usual. And it *did* have something to do with her emotional reaction to Garret. She wasn't afraid to admit that, or even wonder about what it meant. It was so…different and unique she couldn't help but want to explore, study, dissect.

But Shay needed to hear the important truths, told in Betty's usual straightforward, calm way. "You've only lost Holden and Reece. You gained Connor, and Sabrina will be back once she heals. Probably with a vengeance. You didn't lose Elsie. She's just going to be here rather than at headquarters, at *your* suggestion, I might remind you."

"For now," Shay returned darkly.

"Sure, but she'll train her replacements when she decides to leave for good. She'll find someone else just as good at computers."

Shay sighed, studying the sky as a plane came into view. "It feels like we're falling apart, Bet."

"Maybe," Betty agreed. Things were changing. People who'd made North Star their lives for years were learning to build lives and hopes outside of North Star. Right here in the real world, where they might create something rather than constantly risking their necks to save something or someone.

Shay might see it as a falling apart, but Betty saw it as something kind of beautiful. People who'd come to North Star because of vengeance or fear or not having anywhere else to go were building real lives.

Which meant maybe Betty could, too. She eyed her friend. Maybe even Shay could find the peace she so desperately needed. "Maybe we need to fall apart," Betty mused.

Shay looked at her, stricken, but Betty didn't feel shaken or upset by it. Life was change, and loss, and learning new skill sets. "We're not getting any younger, Shay. You and I have been at North Star the longest. We've put our hearts and souls into it and done a lot of good, but what do we have to show for it?"

"Aside from all the not-dead people who are alive because of us?"

"Yes. Something for *us*?"

"Do we have to have something for us?"

"No. Not necessarily, but I think we deserve something."

"I swear to God, Reece brainwashed you all," Shay said, referring to their old operative and friend, who'd exchanged fieldwork for the quiet life a while back.

Betty chuckled, but it quickly died. Shay's gaze went sharp and the world around them went still as smoke began to pour from the aircraft high above them.

"What's going on?" Garret barked. He lurched forward.

Betty stared expectantly at Shay, but she said nothing. Just watched the downward trajectory of the plane.

"We have to do something," Nate said, looking from Shay to Mallory to the plummeting plane. "Why are you just standing there?"

"We have to *do* something," Garret said, repeating Nate's words. Then he started moving forward, jogging toward where the plane hurtled to the ground.

He would run all the way to that crash site and end up hurting himself.

Shay's reaction, though, had Betty questioning what was *really* going on, because usually Shay would be the first to run toward a crashing plane.

"Garret." Betty ran after him and took his arm carefully, because the only one she could manage to reach out and grab was his injured one. "Garret. Stop."

The plane landed, a ways off, with an echoing boom and screech.

"They can't be dead," Garret said, his voice broken.

Betty stared at the sky. No, no, it was too easy. She began to pull Garret back to where Shay, Mallory and Elsie stood looking stoic. While Nate raked his hands through his hair.

Betty gave Shay a look, one that she hoped communicated to Shay that she should tell Garret what the hell was going on. But Shay shook her head. Then she exchanged a glance with Elsie, who nodded slightly.

"Els," Shay said quietly. "I want security video from that airport."

"On it." Elsie disappeared, and Shay conferred with Mallory in low tones Betty couldn't hear.

"It can't be true," Garret said, more insistent this time. He wasn't staring at the smoke. He was glaring at Shay. Who wasn't saying anything. "What the hell is going on? It *can't* be true."

Betty knew Shay wanted to be sure before North Star offered an official stance, but…the guy was wrecked. *Again.*

"It isn't true," Betty said, squeezing his arm gently. "Tell us what's going on, Shay."

# Chapter Three

Garret could only stare at Betty's profile. *It isn't true.* How did she know? How did…? A loud boom echoed through the air, and still no one moved. No one reacted in any way to the plane *exploding*.

Garret felt like he was in a dream. None of this made any sense. He pointed at Shay, because dream or not, she was the head of their secret group. "Explain," he demanded.

"We don't have proof," Shay said in her leader way that irritated the hell out of Garret. He hadn't had someone *leading* him in a very long time.

"Explain," he repeated.

"Shay!" Elsie waved Shay over to where she sat in Nate's truck, tapping away at laptop keys. Shay gave one last look at Garret, said nothing and then marched over to Elsie, Mallory on her heels.

Before he could lunge forward, grab the woman by the shoulders and shake some answers out of her, Betty placed a gentle hand on his.

"Garret. It's too easy. It's too… The grandmother says no. She refuses, refuses, refuses. We're getting lawyers involved. State-mandated paternity tests. She changes her mind, then *oops*, she and the kids die in a plane crash? I don't buy it."

The information cascaded inside of him. It was…a little too easy. But why go through the trouble of a fake plane crash? Agreeing to meet?

"That's what Shay was thinking when she asked Elsie to look at the footage?" Nate asked.

"Yes. A sign they didn't get on the plane, or maybe the planes were switched out. Shay and Mallory didn't have to be here, Garret. Elsie and I were already. Operatives on the ground means they suspected something was up."

"No one thought to tell me?" Garret demanded. There was a rage inside of him—not just at this *group* and their interference, but at Savannah and this whole thing from top to bottom. He knew Betty wasn't the right target for his anger, but he was struggling to beat it back.

"I don't know what's going on. I'm only the doctor. I'm sure they wanted to spare your worries in case they were wrong."

"Oh, you're right. Watching their plane explode wasn't concerning at all." He couldn't keep the sarcasm from his tone.

"Listen, Garret," Nate said, stepping forward and meeting Garret's gaze. "I know this is a terrible situation, but just give me a few minutes. Elsie will tell me what's going on."

"You're so sure about that?"

"Yes," Nate returned evenly. "But let's let her do the work she needs to do to prove those kids weren't on the plane first."

Sirens began to scream through the air. Whatever emergency vehicles had been alerted were heading to the crash site, and Garret stood here outside a private airport with his brother and some woman he barely knew and…

His children could be dead. No matter how nonchalant everyone was, his children could be *dead*.

Betty's hand slid up and down his arm. "Garret, we already know the grandmother doesn't want you to have those kids. It's not a stretch to hope that there might be something more to this plane crash. That they just want you to believe the twins are dead."

Garret jerked his arm away from her reach, then immediately regretted it as a white-hot lance of pain went up his arm. He refused to outwardly react, though his voice was a little more vicious than it needed to be. "Why? If Savannah is dead, why? Even if she was alive, I never did anything to *her*. She betrayed me. Lied to me. Made a fool out of me." Why was *he* the one paying for everyone else's actions?

- Nate made an odd sound as he looked back at Elsie, nose to the laptop screen. There was an expression on his face…a reticence…

"You know something." Garret knew he didn't have a right to feel betrayed by Nate. For years, Garret had believed his brother was suffering PTSD rather than telling the truth about the military corruption he'd recently uncovered with the help of Elsie's group.

But he felt betrayed all the same when Nate stood there. Looking guilty.

"I don't know…anything concrete."

Garret felt as though he'd been punched in the solar plexus. "But you know something," he managed to rasp.

Nate sighed heavily. "Elsie's been looking into Savannah's death."

"Looking into… Why?"

"She just wondered… It was a good hospital she was in, and while the twins were premature, it wasn't… She just wondered if…"

"She thinks Savannah is still alive?"

"It was a theory she was pursuing."

"And everyone knew this except me?"

"No," Nate said, but in a careful way that made it hard for Garret to believe.

"Clearly Shay knew enough to be here. To bring *backup*."

"Shay's Elsie's boss. She had to tell Shay."

"And you, because you're her boyfriend, but not me. The man who Savannah *actually* used. The man who is supposed to be the father of those kids. *Me*, the person whose life this messes up?"

"I'm sorry, Garret. We're doing the best we can here. We didn't want to… *I* didn't want to… Savannah faking her death sounds crazy." Nate didn't have to say the rest. *And you've already thought I was crazy once.*

When would this nightmare end?

"Just stay put," Nate said. "Let me see what Elsie's got."

Nate walked off toward Elsie and her coworkers. Garret didn't move. He couldn't. Too much was happening.

But he was a cop. Had been for fifteen years. He'd

been in difficult, confusing and morally ambiguous situations before.

He had to get past his personal connection. Focus on what he was going to do.

Savannah. Alive? Why would she want those kids? *His* kids. She'd never mentioned wanting kids. Never mentioned not wanting them. And he'd been so pre-occupied with setting up Blue Valley's PD and...

No, there was no point in going back over it. She'd been conning him anyway. So, the past didn't matter now. Only the future did. Only those kids did. *If* Savannah was alive... If she had them...

He studied Betty. She was no operative, not like Shay and Mallory. She was all cut-and-dried science.

But it turned out that was what he needed in this moment. Not some secret group. Only his own two hands, and someone to tell him if those babies were okay.

He glanced at the truck where Shay, Mallory, Elsie and Nate conferred. About what was going on with *his* life. Not theirs. He looked down at Betty, who was watching him. Almost as if she felt sorry for him, which he didn't care for, but at least it was a feeling instead of cool detachment.

He'd take it. He'd use it.

"I'm going to go get my kids. And you're coming with me."

BETTY DID NOT trust the look in Garret's eyes. There was a wildness. A desperation. Those things never led anywhere *good*.

"Garret."

He took her by the wrist and began to lead her toward his truck. She didn't resist. She'd learned long ago she did better with words than she'd ever do with physical displays.

She followed him all the way to his truck. Shay and the rest huddled around Elsie's computer, not paying attention to the man who was really at the center of this.

She knew they meant well. North Star wanted to complete the mission, get Garret his kids. They wanted to help and do the right thing. But they were so used to…doing, not helping those caught in the cross fire.

Betty knew a little too much about the cross fire.

When he stopped at his truck, he opened the passenger-side door and pointed at the seat as if he expected her to just climb in.

"Are you kidnapping me?" she asked coolly, folding her arms over her chest.

"I could, I suppose, but no. I'm going, Betty. You can either get in and come with me and help, or you can go back to your group. But you're not going to stop me."

Betty knew she should go back to Shay. Shay and Mallory would catch up with Garret in no time. They'd help him no matter what fuss he put up, and hopefully get him out of the fray so he could *heal*.

But he was…holding on by a thread. He needed someone to be the voice of reason. And it looked like for today it was going to have to be her.

She climbed into the passenger seat, somewhat rewarded by the fact he seemed shocked she'd agreed to go with him. But he got over his surprise quickly, skirted his truck front and climbed into the driver's seat.

"So, where are we going, then?" she asked.

"I know where Savannah would go to hide if she's alive."

"If she knows you know this hiding place of hers, why would she—"

"She doesn't know. Believe me, she doesn't have a clue the things I know about her now."

## Chapter Four

Garret knew he needed to find some inner calm. He'd been trained to control his emotions, and to make snap decisions with as little human reaction as possible.

But no matter what training he'd had or how many years he'd been a police officer, he *was* human.

Betty's calm in the passenger seat should center him. Remind him that he needed to stop, think and plan. Certainly not go off on a wild-goose chase for his dead ex-wife.

They thought she was alive. Betty's group thought Savannah was alive and it was bad enough she'd hidden *his* children from him, but to still be alive in the aftermath...

Meanwhile Betty sat there, cool as a cucumber, as if they were taking a lazy Sunday drive. Because *she* wanted to.

"Do you just get kidnapped every day?" he demanded, negotiating a curve too fast. He knew he should ease up. He'd dealt with the aftermath of people who did not ease up on these dangerous mountain roads.

Her words were devoid of any kind of reaction. "It's cute that you think I was kidnapped."

He frowned over at her before returning his gaze to the road. Her expression had been that obnoxious blankness he recognized so well because he had to adopt it on his job, too. And this *was* a job for her. That was all.

It was his life.

"What do you call it if not kidnapping?"

"I'm no operative, Garret, but I know how to protect myself. You didn't force me to be here. Nor could you have done anything to stop me."

"Because I've got a gunshot wound in my shoulder thanks to your little group?"

"Because you wouldn't really be able to force someone to do something for very long because deep down you're too honorable. Which I predict you're going to bluster over, but at your core, you want to—maybe *have* to—do what's right."

"No one has to do what's right, and honorable people are driven to do dishonorable things all the time."

"I suppose people can be," she said after a while, softly. "But it isn't you, Garret." She turned to face him, this woman who shouldn't know him so well. "I want to help," she said firmly. "I want to help you meet your children. It isn't right that they've been kept from you, and at the end of the day, my job is to do what's right."

"Even if it means going against your boss?"

"Shay will understand." She said it firmly, but he wondered if deep down she wasn't so sure.

Garret kept driving. He wasn't sure what to say to her. What to do with voluntary help. All he knew was he had to find Savannah, and the secret cabin he'd discovered when he'd investigated her after she'd left him.

Maybe she'd taken his children and jetted off to Siberia. Maybe she really was dead and his children had gone down on that plane. A whole lot of *maybes*.

But one of those *maybes* was that Savannah was secreted away in her tiny cabin high in the Rocky Mountains.

"If we played this with a little more tact and patience—"

"If they're expecting us to believe that plane crash, it's not just to fake kill off my children. They could have done that any number of ways. That crash was meant to be a diversion. Tact and patience is going to lead us to a cold, dead end."

She didn't speak, and Garret got the feeling that meant she agreed with him. No matter how reluctantly.

So he focused on the road as it got more narrow, and more treacherous. He'd gone up here only once before, in a fog after Savannah had left, leaving evidence of more than one affair in her wake. There'd been an anger inside of him then. One that had scared him enough to try to control.

But there had been times when the unknowns and the fury had gotten the better of him, and he'd looked into every facet of Savannah's background in an attempt to dissect and understand what had happened.

He'd found this off-the-grid cabin in her records, owned by somebody who didn't really exist as far as Garret had been able to find. But the deed had been there, in a small box of papers Barney had dug up in the backyard.

Garret couldn't imagine he'd been supposed to find that one. Maybe he was wrong. Maybe he was wrong about everything.

But he didn't slow down. Some things had to be seen

through to the end, even if he *was* wrong. Because his children were at stake. He'd go down a million wrong roads to find the right one.

"Are you going to go screeching up to this mysterious place your dead wife might be or do you plan to slow down before arrival?" Betty asked.

Her calm should have irritated him, but the delivery devoid of any blame or judgment had the opposite effect. He eased his foot off the pedal, though he didn't stop.

"We've got a ways to go yet."

"Why don't you tell me where we're going?"

"So you can report to your team?"

She laughed, and if he wasn't reaching there was just a hint of derision in her tone. "If you'll recall, you grabbed me. All of my belongings are still at that airfield, or in your cabin."

He frowned. "You don't have your phone?"

"No, I handed it to Elsie for her to do an update thing while we waited."

"It wouldn't work up here anyway."

"Haven't you learned anything about North Star yet?"

He didn't know how to answer that. Elsie and her crew had always been very careful not to mention the name of their secret group, but North Star had to be it. Betty didn't even seem to think it needed to be a secret.

It shouldn't make him pause or think, but the realization she didn't have a way to contact anyone made him...uneasy. Like he'd done something wrong—even though she'd come willingly and even argued when he'd called it kidnapping. The fact she'd given the secret name away—because she was a *doctor*, not an operative—made him rethink his actions back there at the airfield.

Where a plane had exploded. If not with his children on it, then because he was supposed to think his children were on it.

"Your group… They don't make mistakes, right?"

"Everyone makes mistakes, Garret," Betty said gently. "But I doubt very much they made a mistake by being there today. I don't think they'd believe no one was on that plane if it didn't have a very strong possibility of being true."

Garret nodded as he negotiated another hairpin curve. "It doesn't make sense that they need to go through all this effort to make me think they're dead— even their grandmother. She had a right to those kids. They were left with her. I wasn't named as father—hell, Savannah made it quite clear I wasn't the only man she was sleeping with when we were married." Garret gripped the steering wheel even harder if that was possible. He didn't like to think or talk about what a fool he'd been, but it was important to acknowledge. "They might not be mine."

"Maybe. But Savannah's cousin said they were. Maybe she's wrong, but…"

"That doesn't make sense, either."

"Sometimes things don't make sense. You have a pile of disparate pieces you need to put together—not how you want to, not how you think they should go together, but how they *do*. We just don't have enough pieces yet."

"So what the hell do we do?"

"Keep collecting them until we find enough to figure this mystery out."

BETTY WAS FEELING a little green not much later. The higher altitude and curves would be a recipe for car sickness for anyone, and she'd never done particularly well with heights.

Garret had slowed down his manic pace, but he didn't stop pushing the speed limit. That urgency was palpable. Along with all the underlying emotions it cloaked…

Pain. Betrayal. Uncertainty.

Why did he have to be good-looking *and* emotionally and physically wounded? Honestly, a woman could only resist so much before she started weaving fantasies.

Which were a lot better than the queasiness in her stomach anyway. She'd seen him without his shirt, sewed him up, bandaged and rebandaged him and administered medical care. She could come up with *quite* a few fantasies even with her rather scientific, mathematically-minded imagination.

But her fantasies were interrupted when Garret slowed the truck. He was coming to a stop because even his truck wouldn't take them through the giant snowpack covering the road—if it could even be called a road—in front of them.

"Well, this is a problem," Betty offered.

"Not exactly." He turned and began to reach behind him before he hissed out a breath, clearly hurting his shoulder. He let out a grunt and got out of the truck. He jerked the back door open with his good arm and pulled out a backpack. "You're not dressed for this, so just stay put."

"Stay put?"

"In the truck. I won't be long."

"Where on earth are you going?" Before she'd even gotten the question out, he'd closed the door. The truck was still running, heat pouring out of the vents and keeping her warm. She should let him hike off to wherever he was going to go. He was dressed for the cold better than she was, and had some kind of pack of supplies. She doubted he would leave her here with the truck running if he was going to be gone for long. He might not be thinking clearly, but he was a smart guy not liable to strand them on top of a dang mountain.

She *hoped*.

Shaking her head—not sure if she was more irritated with him or herself—Betty reached over and turned the ignition off. She pocketed the keys, zipped up her coat and then braved the cold and snow. Luckily she was wearing boots. She had dressed for winter—but not *deep, upper-elevation* winter.

Immediately she was thrust into a blinding white world of icy cold, but it made it easy to follow Garret. He'd left a trail of footprints in the snow. Somehow going even higher up.

Betty didn't look around her. Some people might enjoy the awe-inspiring view from atop a mountain. Betty much preferred the *bottom*.

When she finally caught up with Garret he was lying prone on a slab of snow that seemed to jut out over nothing but thin air below. Just the sight of him that close to what was likely a long drop made her stomach plummet.

"I said stay put," he growled without looking at her. He held binoculars and didn't pull his face away as he spoke, just kept looking at whatever he was looking at.

"You can order me around all you like. It won't make me follow said orders." Betty stayed far away from the ledge he was lying on. "What are you doing?"

He got up out of the snow and walked over to her. He handed her the binoculars he'd been holding. He pointed into the distance below. Betty took the binoculars, wincing at how cold they were against her bare hands. She knew she'd have to get closer to the edge to see what he wanted her to see.

She looked at the edge of whatever kind of cliff they were on, then looked at Garret. He was covered in snow. There was even some in the scruffy beard he'd been growing since shaving hurt with his shoulder wound.

Betty had spent far too many mornings charting its growth and had, luckily, resisted the urge to offer to shave it for him.

"Afraid of heights?" he asked with a raised eyebrow.

She didn't consider herself an overly prideful person, or even particularly contentious like most of the people she worked with at North Star. She was comfortable in her own skin and didn't need to prove anything to anyone.

But the word *afraid* apparently made all those simple truths she'd always thought about herself evaporate. She took three defiant steps toward the ledge, then looked through the binoculars in the direction he had pointed.

A cabin came into view. Nothing like the small, rustic fishing cabin where Betty had patched Garret up after his gunshot wound. It wasn't large, but it was…

slick. A bit like a magazine ad, out here in the middle of nowhere with nothing but mountains and snow around them.

Beyond that, smoke curled upward from the chimney. There were no vehicles in the snow, but tire tracks led to a garage.

"Do you think that's her?" Betty asked, handing him the binoculars, then taking steps far away from the edge again.

"I don't know, but I know she owns this place."

"Couldn't someone have bought it after she died?"

"Maybe," Garret said, and though he didn't look through the binoculars again, he stared in the cabin's direction.

"So what are we going to do?"

He didn't say anything for long, cold seconds. Betty waited. And waited. "We could wait for Shay to show up," she offered. "You know she will do just that."

Garret scowled. "Maybe."

"Not maybe. She will."

"Okay, she will. I don't want your group crashing into this."

"They only want to help."

"I'm grateful for the help you guys gave Nate. And you gave me," he said, gesturing at his shoulder. "I am. Sincerely. But everything your group did for Nate raised a lot of unanswered questions for me. I realize North Star might want to help me answer them, but I have to figure some things out on my own."

She didn't try to talk him out of his conclusions.

"I'll start hiking," he said, stowing his binoculars and tightening his pack. He winced because those straps should *not* be on a gunshot wound. "You're sure Shay will reach you? I'll leave you here with the truck and my phone. You can start driving back down and—"

"I'm sorry. What?"

"You're not dressed for a hike. It's too cold. You're a liability if I can't drive closer." He pointed back from where they'd come.

"You're a liability to yourself with that gunshot wound. You shouldn't be wearing that backpack. You're not up for this, Garret. We'll both go back down and—"

"I'll be fine."

God save her from stubborn men. "I can guarantee you, you won't. You might survive, but you're risking all sorts of things. Further injury. Infection. I'm not even considering what the elements might do to you when you're incapacitated."

"I'm on my own two legs, aren't I?"

"You didn't get shot in the leg, though perhaps it would have been better if you had. I'm sorry. I can't allow you to go off gallivanting in subzero temperatures with that injury. You will wind up dead. Beginning and end of story."

Garret crossed his arms over his chest, sizing her up. "How do you plan on stopping me?"

Betty sighed. She didn't want to have to play this game, but he wasn't going to be sensible. Which meant she was going to have to show him just how she planned to stop him cold.

## Chapter Five

Garret did not care for the expression on Betty's face. It wasn't one of her bland clinical looks. It wasn't even that vague disapproving expression she got sometimes when he was being particularly stubborn.

This was narrow-eyed determination.

"At least let me take the pack," she offered, and though her face was arranged in a different way, that voice was familiar. Calm. Detached. Maybe vaguely accommodating. "I know you need supplies, but you simply can't do that to your shoulder. Maybe I can rejig it so it's resting on your good shoulder only."

He frowned a little. The calm offer was more in keeping with how she usually acted, but that flinty-eyed stare made him uneasy.

She moved toward him, and what was he going to do? Back away? Fight her off? Of course not. Besides, she wasn't going to—

His good arm was jerked behind his back and it was complete and utter shock that she'd actually…moved on him. Was trying to incapacitate him.

It took nothing at all to sidestep, swivel and have his arm back out straight again. But he didn't know what to do next because he wasn't going to…fight this woman. "What are you going to do? Drag me back to the truck?"

She shrugged. This time when she moved, he could see her tell and he did sidestep it. She moved around him, like a boxer in a ring, and he moved with her— keeping her in front of him.

"Stop this. It's a waste of time. You aren't cut out for the cold. Go back to the truck and—"

"Not without you. You're not physically capable of what you want to do right now. As your doctor—"

"You're fired."

She chuckled at that, still walking in slow circles around him. "This is childish," he said, putting enough *cop* in his tone to hopefully get through to her.

Instead, she feinted right, but he saw through it and didn't fall for it. She lunged at him, and she knew his weaknesses—what with being the woman who'd stitched up and managed his bad side—and his instincts didn't quite account for the wound in his shoulder.

She got a kick in that took him down to a knee. He had no idea what she thought she was going to do with him even if she *did* incapacitate him—but they weren't going to get to that point.

He popped back onto two feet, swiveled out of her grasp and away from the handcuffs she'd pulled from… somewhere. "Should I even ask why you have hand-cuffs on you?"

"Just because I'm a doctor doesn't mean I don't know how to incapacitate someone. You'd be surprised how many men simply refuse to take good care of themselves because of their fragile egos."

"You're not going to get those handcuffs on me." He

knew he shouldn't say the next part, but the words fell out anyway. "And my ego is hardly fragile."

"I think I might get these handcuffs on you. It might take a while, and it won't be easy, but it can and will be done if you don't see some sense. You're only going to hurt yourself trying to stop me," she said with total confidence and a straight face. This tiny little woman.

"I'm only going to hurt *you*."

She had the nerve to grin at him. "Yeah, right. You don't have it in you, Garret. Not because of the injury—because of your moral code. Now—"

He heard the quiet click somewhere in the distance and moved before he even thought of it, tackling her into the snow and keeping her safe underneath him as the sound of a gunshot exploded in the air.

Garret stayed there, protecting Betty's body with his even as the cold seeped in around them. He kept his breathing slow and listened, turning his head to the side to study their surroundings.

But there was nothing but silence. And they couldn't stay here forever. Someone had shot at them. He looked down at her. Her eyes were wide, but she didn't move to push him off or anything. She just lay there. Scared, clearly.

He didn't have time for scared. He rolled off Betty, trying to bite back a groan against the familiar pain in his shoulder. He'd moved too fast, leaned too hard on that side. He didn't have time for this injury, either.

"Are you okay?" Betty asked, sitting up from her prone position in the snow. She looked around as he did, searching for whoever had shot at them.

"I'm fine," Garret gritted out, the pain of his shoulder radiating through his entire body. But someone had shot at them. From where? Below? How could anyone see them up here? "I'm not sure where they shot from. I just heard…" He frowned at her, sitting there covered in snow, pink cheeked and shivering.

This had gotten completely out of hand and it was entirely his fault. He could see it clearly now. From the moment he'd heard he might have children out there, he hadn't made a solid decision. It had upended his entire life.

Even though he hadn't yet met them. He still hadn't…

He shook his head. He could only focus on one problem at a time and right now the person shooting at them had to be his top priority. He had to remember how to compartmentalize and actually make the right decision.

"Stay low," he ordered. This time, he had a feeling Betty would actually listen. On his belly, he pulled himself through the snow to the ledge. The only sign of life had been that cabin below. The shot *had* to have come from there.

He looked over the edge, keeping his head as hidden as possible. The cabin was far off, but he could see someone standing outside it. Someone with a gun, pointed in their general direction.

It was Savannah. Even without his binoculars he knew it. She was a small figure with the distance between them, but he recognized the way she held herself, the blond hair underneath the black stocking cap. The height, the weight. He might not be able to make out her features, but he had no doubts the woman standing in front of the cabin was Savannah.

She'd shot at them. Was currently studying the

cliff they were on, her gun poised and ready to shoot again. Garret scooted away from the edge, ignoring the screaming pain in his shoulder.

"What is it?" Betty whispered from somewhere behind him.

"My dead ex-wife. With a gun."

BETTY SHOULDN'T BE SURPRISED. After all, wasn't this Shay and Elsie's theory anyway? That Savannah Loren was still alive. Garret had come here because he thought this was where she might be. It all made sense.

Even the shooting at them part. Except... "How would she know we're up here?"

"I don't know." Garret studied their surroundings, and she could tell he was struggling to stay in this moment. To deal with the problem at hand. Because Savannah wasn't supposed to be alive, and no matter what had happened in their marriage, Betty imagined he hadn't expected his ex-wife to shoot at him. Especially from the dead.

"We need Shay," Betty said. She knew he wouldn't like it, but one injured cop and one freezing-cold doctor could hardly take on people with guns.

He shook his head. "We need a plan."

"Shay is the plan. She has the tactical experience. She has...everything."

"I've got some tactical experience of my own."

"As a small-town cop?" she demanded, hearing the slight shrill note in her voice. She was panicking and that just wouldn't do. Maybe she wasn't a field operative, and maybe she didn't usually get put in a position to be shot at, but she was hardly a regular civilian.

Even before she'd joined North Star, her life had not been easy or free of danger. She...

"Yeah, as a small-town cop," he retorted coldly.

It was the chill in his voice that had her closing her eyes and taking a breath. Garret was grumpy and could take his irritation out on those around him, but he was never cold. Things had gotten out of hand, and she needed to get ahold of herself.

And stop shrieking things at him when they were in this together. Shay would get here. Whether Garret wanted North Star's help or not, he was going to get it. They just had to wait it out.

"I'm going down there."

"Garret."

"She's not going to kill me. She could have when I didn't know she was alive. So, I'm going to go down there. You're going to get in the truck and drive back to Blue Valley and tell Shay and whoever what's going on."

"You don't know she's not going to shoot you, Garret."

"No, I don't. But I can't walk away from this."

"And I can't walk away from you. You brought me here, Garret. You involved me. You can't just send me away now. If she won't shoot you, why would she shoot me if I'm *with* you?"

"It's too long of a hike for you in those clothes."

Betty sat in the snow, cold all the way through but pretending like she was in a dang sauna. She crossed her arms over her chest and raised one eyebrow, keeping her tone calm and detached. "Okay, that's fine. We can stay up here arguing until Shay and the team get here."

He scowled at her. "Fine," he muttered. He crouched

and moved away from the edge, then, once he could stand at his full height without being seen from below, he started marching down the way they'd come.

Betty tried not to smile her triumph. Being persistent *always* paid off. She followed him down back to the truck. He jerked open the back door and then pulled out a duffel bag. He pulled out a sweatshirt and some thick socks.

"The extra boots won't fit, even if you load up on socks."

"I'll ball up the socks and put them in the toe. That should work."

He blinked at her, then shrugged. "Go for it. Layer up. Make sure you can still move—climb, jump, run." He moved out of the way and she pawed through his belongings to put the far-too-big clothes on. She was still wet from lying in the snow, but this was a temporary solution.

She pulled a stocking cap over her hair and then slid some gloves on. They were so big it was comical, but they would do the trick.

He studied her when she turned to him. "You'll do," he grumbled, then slammed the truck door. "Come on, then."

He started marching toward the large snowbank, and Betty had no choice but to follow. She wasn't sure how long they'd walked when she started to realize she'd handled this all wrong. She should have stayed in the truck. With heat. She should have driven back to Shay and let North Star take care of this.

What had she been *thinking*?

"Doing okay back there?"

"Just fine," Betty retorted, doing everything she could to keep the bitterness and fatigue out of her voice.

"Sure," Garret replied, almost sounding amused. She scowled at his back.

Eventually, his pace slowed and she could tell he was taking great pains not to be heard. They had to be getting close.

As they climbed over a snowdrift, the cabin came into view. A tall, blonde woman stood in front of the house, a gun in her hands, though it was pointed at the ground. She stared up at the mountain cliff where Garret and Betty had been.

Had she been standing out here waiting the whole time? Even with the extra layers, Betty was freezing. This woman was wearing a sweater and that was it.

Garret had them situated so they were hidden by the snowdrift. He looked back at her, dark eyes blank and unreadable. She had no idea what he was planning and suddenly her heart drummed in her chest—not just because she was exhausted, but because that look was… haunting.

"Stay here, hidden by the snow," he said in a low voice. Then he stepped into the clearing in front of the drift. "Savannah?"

The woman whirled, gun at the ready. Garret stepped into the clearing, arms up. "It'd be easier if you didn't shoot me."

"Garret," the woman said. If she saw Betty, she made no mention of it. Her eyes were wide and solely focused on Garret's large form.

Betty held herself rigid and ready to act. She didn't know what Garret thought he was doing moving toward a woman with a gun when he'd already been shot once, and not that long ago, but he clearly understood Savannah or the situation because slowly Savannah lowered the gun to point at the ground again.

Garret kept moving toward her, and it didn't *look* like she was going to shoot him, but it took everything inside of Betty to stay where she was. To trust Garret to handle this. Savannah was his ex-wife after all. He was a cop. He knew what he was doing.

"Garret," Savannah said again. She shook her head but then a big smile broke out on her face. "Oh, my God, it's you!" And then the tall blonde launched herself at him.

# *Chapter Six*

Garret caught Savannah without thinking. A woman threw her body at a man, he had to catch it whether he wanted to or not.

He didn't *want*. She was supposed to be dead. She'd cheated on him when she was alive. Worst of all, she'd had his children and never let him know. He knew he should *hate* this woman, but his feelings weren't that simple. Whatever love there had been was gone, but it hadn't soured fully into hate.

Not yet.

He set her on her feet and tried to gently nudge her away but she reached up and cupped his face with her hands, looking up at him like she was happy to see him. "I can't believe you're here. You're real."

"Me?" When she was the one who was supposed to be dead.

Her smile didn't falter. Her blue eyes sparkled. He'd once thought that look was tears she was holding in check, but he didn't trust anything he'd once thought about her anymore.

"I'd hoped you'd find me, but you're not one to look past the circumstantial evidence, are you?"

She said it with a smile, like it was a compliment or endearment. But it wasn't. In the aftermath of her leaving him, Garret had combed over every second of their relationship, beginning to end, and even before he'd found out she'd played him the whole time—that she'd been sent to undercut any confidence he might have had in his brother's tales about military corruption—he'd known she'd played him, and often.

Little jabs said with a smile. Volatile mood swings meant to keep him off guard and always used to assign him blame.

"Where are my children?"

Something changed in her gaze, and she finally seemed to understand he wasn't glad. Not to see her alive or at all. She dropped her hands. "I didn't realize…"

"That I knew?"

"That that's all you cared about."

A well of anger filled him. Dark and hot, but it was familiar. He'd felt it in those first days after learning of her infidelity. He'd controlled it then. He was well adept at controlling it now.

But something had Savannah looking over his shoulder to where Betty would have been out of sight. Garret immediately reached out and grasped Savannah's gun arm. "She's with me."

Savannah looked up at him, one of those cold looks he well remembered from those times they fought. Rare, but always vicious. "Is she?"

"I want to see my children, Savannah."

Something passed over her face and Garret didn't trust himself to name it, because it looked like grief.

Or guilt. But neither would work on him. He couldn't let them. She'd hurt him in every way possible—except physically—and despite holding on to him, she still also held on to her gun.

Betty came to stand next to him. She said nothing, even as his hand remained on Savannah's arm. Because he felt the tension there. No, she didn't want to shoot him—but for whatever reason, she wasn't so sure about Betty.

"Betty's a doctor. I brought her here to give the children a checkup so I'd know they're safe and healthy."

Her eyes flashed to his. "I didn't want children, but I'm not a monster."

"I guess that depends on how you define *monster*."

"You have no idea—*no* idea—what I've had to do, to survive. To keep my children safe."

"Garret. Savannah. This is such a strange circumstance," Betty said gently, but without a saccharine sympathy that might have put his or Savannah's back up. "There are a lot of moving parts and it looks like neither of you fully know the truth about what's going on. Maybe we could go inside and talk it out."

"I won't let someone who thinks I'm the villain into my home."

"You lied to me from day one, trying to make me believe my brother was insane. You faked your own death in a way that made sure I'd never know about my children. You don't get to play the victim, Savannah."

"And you do?"

"Petty fighting doesn't help anyone," Betty said in that brisk manner that reminded him of a kindergarten teacher. "Regardless as to who has a right to it. Savannah, if you don't want us to go inside—"

She jerked her arm away from Garret and Garret immediately stepped in front of Betty. He wasn't about to have her caught in the cross fire of something that he shouldn't have involved her in.

Savannah rolled her eyes. "Relax, supercop. I'm not going to shoot her. Come inside." She waved them toward the cabin.

Garret glanced at Betty. He wasn't sure she should walk into this, but he didn't know what else to do with her. She should have gone back to the truck the million times he'd told her to. He should have *forced* her to stay at the truck.

But he couldn't keep beating himself up for all the things he *should* have done. There was only now.

"Stay behind me. Watch the gun," he murmured to Betty before he followed Savannah toward the cabin.

Betty didn't respond, but he didn't have time to impress upon her how important listening to him was now. He could only lead her into the lion's den and hope he had the means to tame the lion.

He glanced at Savannah's back as she disappeared inside. She'd hugged him and touched him like she was happy to see him. He didn't know what to make of it, but he knew better than to trust it.

He'd never trust any move she made ever again. That was something he'd promise himself here and now.

Once inside, Savannah kept moving into the cabin. To a hallway. "Stay here," he muttered to Betty. "By the door." Just in case she needed to escape.

The hallway was dark and Savannah opened the door

to a room. She gestured him inside. He knew it could be a trap. There were a million rational thoughts telling him to turn around. Anything to protect himself.

But something kept moving him forward. When he looked into the room, it was dim but not completely dark. And it was…a baby room.

*Babies.*

There was a crib in the corner and Garret's heartbeat was so hard in his ears he couldn't think beyond it. Just *boom, boom, boom* as he moved forward, propelled by something outside himself. Because inwardly, he was nothing. Empty. A ghost, maybe.

When he looked into the crib, there were two babies, fast asleep.

He felt like gravity had been upended. The crushing pressure in his chest was almost too much to breathe through. They both slept, back-to-back, curled up in the same exact position. One had a shock of dark hair, the other had less hair and in a lighter brunette.

He couldn't move. He wasn't sure he could breathe, and when someone touched him, he somehow knew it was Betty. Not Savannah.

"Breathe, Garret. They're beautiful. Everything's going to be all right."

It brought him back to the moment. To the reality. Yes, his babies being right here within reach rearranged… everything inside him.

But it didn't change reality.

He looked back at Savannah, whose arms were crossed as she narrow-eyed Betty.

He wasn't convinced everything was all right, but he was going to make sure it was. For his children.

BETTY FELT TEARS sting her eyes. It was foolishly emotional, but the way Garret had looked down at those precious babies like they were the water he'd desperately been seeking in a long desert journey…it made her heart mush.

"They're…okay, aren't they?" he asked in a whisper, still staring at them as though they might disappear like a mirage.

"Of course they're okay," Savannah snapped from behind them. "My grandmother's been taking excellent care of them."

Betty watched Garret's face turn a little harder. As if snapping back into the real world and all they still faced.

"Where's your mother?"

"She'll be back eventually," Savannah said. When Betty glanced at her, she was staring daggers in Betty's direction.

"I'll check them out once they wake up," Betty said. She realized she hadn't taken her hand off his arm, so she patted it awkwardly. "Let's let them sleep."

Garret nodded and reluctantly backed away from the crib. He didn't break his gaze from their sleeping forms until the wall physically made it impossible.

Savannah led them to a cozy living room. There was a fire crackling in the fireplace. Blankets and rugs and comfortable furniture. It was a nice place to live— and hide.

"Go ahead and sit."

Garret looked around the room with distrustful eyes. But he eventually took a seat on a couch and nodded for Betty to sit down next to him.

Savannah frowned at that, but Betty couldn't understand why Savannah would think Garret would be *nice* to her. Ever.

"What is this, Savannah?" Garret asked. He was all cop. A man questioning a suspect. Not an ex. Not a father desperate to hold his children.

"It's lots of things." Savannah blew out a breath and for a moment she looked… Betty couldn't drum up any sympathy for the woman, but she looked tired.

"Faking my own death was the only way to get out from under my grandfather's thumb. Yes, I worked for him. Did his bidding. It paid well and he was always kinder to me than my own father was."

"His bidding including marrying me."

Savannah leaned forward in her chair, eyes glowing and intense. "I was sent to Blue Valley to befriend you, yes. Maybe even get you to fall for me. So you would believe what I said about Nate. To undermine Nate and watch for anyone who might start to believe him. I did all that. I can't deny it. But I didn't have to marry you, Garret. I didn't have to have the relationship we had. I wanted that. I love you."

The lack of past tense had something in Betty's chest clutching. She looked at Garret. His expression hadn't changed, but something had. In the charge of the air. Deep inside him somewhere.

"So you cheated on me. Left. Signed the divorce papers. Then faked your own death."

"I had to. Grandfather insisted. It was the worst thing I've ever had to do, and it was when I knew I had to get out. When I found out I was pregnant, I saw my way out."

Garret stood, abruptly. Betty knew he wanted to

pace, but he kept himself still. Energy and pain pumping off him in waves.

She wished she could do something but Savannah's plaintive expression moved from Garret to Betty and immediately went…icy. She clearly saw Betty as some kind of rival, and Betty didn't know how to say she wasn't. Not when this woman…

Betty didn't trust her.

"Your grandparents were taking care of…"

Betty watched Garret grapple with the words. Abruptly he sat back down. "They had the children. And I'm supposed to believe—"

"My grandmother isn't a bad person, Garret. She's on my side. Her taking care of the babies was proof. Proof I was really dead if Grandmother took the children. Grandfather wouldn't be suspicious, but then Grandfather was arrested and we were free."

"Your cousin was also arrested. She had a lot to say about you."

Savannah paused. "Courtney's always been unstable, Garret. Surely anyone who'd ever come into contact with her would know that."

"How do you know I have?"

"I don't. I was only saying. I don't know anything. I've been hiding, Garret. Hiding where I hoped you might eventually find me. You don't think I left that information about this property on accident, do you?"

Betty wanted to believe Savannah was lying, but it was so smooth. So instinctual. It *felt* like the truth, and Betty couldn't understand why that truth made her so uneasy.

A cry sounded through a staticky speaker next to Savannah. She sighed and got up, but Garret was faster. "We'll get them." He held out his hand and Betty took it. The physical connection felt alarmingly…intimate.

When this wasn't intimacy. It was Garret needing to know his children were healthy.

"You'll stay here," he said to Savannah. A clear directive to sit back down.

"You can't tell me what to do in my own home," Savannah returned, full of outrage. "With my own children."

"You'll stay here," Garret repeated, everything about him hard and cold enough Betty thought even Savannah wouldn't cross him.

# Chapter Seven

Garret walked back down the hall, and he kept Betty's hand in his. He didn't need to. He knew that, yet he couldn't let it go. It was a connection to reality when none of what was happening felt real.

A far cry from when he'd first met Betty—when her presence had felt like a reminder of all the ways his life had flipped upside down. It seemed that was all he had anymore—the constant changing of everything he thought he was or wanted.

Because everything paled in the face of becoming a father. He stepped into the room, the small crying sound getting louder as they approached the crib.

The boy was the one making the noise, though the crying stopped as he peered up at Garret. The girl didn't make a peep. She blinked up at him, big dark eyes that seemed to see right into him. A connection. She didn't cry, she didn't smile, just for precious moments met his gaze with hers.

The little boy began to cry again and Garret found himself at an utter loss. His children. *His.* And he didn't know... He didn't even know how to hold them, help them.

But Betty's hand was in his. She would know. Right now she was his anchor.

"Should I…"

"Why don't you pick up the boy. He's fussy," Betty suggested gently.

"I don't know how to… I've never held a baby. My… shoulder."

Betty leaned over the crib edge and picked up the baby. He immediately quieted. "Just like this," she instructed, angling her body to show Garret how it was done. Then she held the boy out and Garret didn't know how to arrange himself, but Betty somehow guided him into it. All in a way that didn't hurt his injured shoulder. So that there was a child in his arms.

*His* child. *His* son.

The boy's face relaxed a little so that his expression looked more like the girl's. Calm. Seeking.

*His*.

"I don't even know their names," he said, his voice coming out raspy and strangled. His children. And he knew nothing about them. Not even how to move forward.

"Cain is the boy. Maggie is the girl," Savannah said from where she stood in the doorway.

It took Garret a while to break his gaze from the boy in his arms. To look up from this miracle to the woman who'd birthed these children. His children.

Savannah was scowling at Betty, who was holding the girl. Maggie. Cain and Maggie. His children.

That Savannah had kept from him. No matter what was going on right now, she had kept these babies from him for months. *Months*.

She had no right to scowl at Betty. She had no right to stand there and act like she was somehow the victim.

Garret walked over to where she stood in the doorway. He grasped the door with his free hand, though it sent a twinge of pain through his shoulder. He looked right at her. "You'll leave us alone until I'm ready to talk to you calmly," he said through gritted teeth. Then he closed the door. In her face. He flipped the lock. He didn't know how to deal with Savannah yet, but for these precious moments he wouldn't. He would meet his children.

"They need to be changed," Betty said softly. She poked through a set of drawers, and then opened the closet. She found diapers and wipes, then studied the room around them. "Grab a blanket from that drawer and spread it out on the floor."

Garret didn't know what to do but obey. He got the blanket and laid it out, holding Cain carefully in his free arm.

Betty knelt on the ground and carefully laid Maggie on the blanket. The girl fussed a little bit, wiggling with her newfound freedom. Betty clearly knew…everything. How to change a diaper. How to hold a baby. How to move through this event that made no earthly sense.

She was unsnapping Maggie's clothes when she nodded at him. "Go ahead and lay Cain down. He'll need a change, too, and there's room."

"I don't know how to do…any of this."

Betty waved that away. "You'll learn. No one's born knowing how to take care of a baby, Garret. Don't be so hard on yourself. Just lay him down and watch what I do and try to replicate it. It'll take some practice."

Garret didn't think there was any chance he'd be able to replicate what Betty was doing, but he was a father. He had to try. He unsnapped Cain's clothes and pulled them up over his stomach. He laid out the new diaper, took off the old. He watched Betty's movements and tried to mirror them exactly.

When he was finished he studied Cain, and then Maggie. "Yours looks better than mine."

She smiled. "Practice." She reached over and tightened the little tabs on Cain's diaper. "There."

"You've changed a lot of diapers?"

"Enough," she said cryptically, resnapping Maggie's onesie. So Garret did the same on Cain's. "I'd like to check them out more thoroughly, but from a basic observation, they look healthy. So you can relax on that score."

"Good. Good." Garret sat back on his heels and looked at his children. *His children.* Why did it feel like being bowled over, again and again, as if he'd never find his footing in this new reality?

"Do you trust her?" Betty asked the question casually.

But it wasn't a casual question. It was weighted with too many things to name.

"No." He had no idea what any of this was. He was too shaken by the kids…by Savannah being alive. By *everything.* But he didn't trust Savannah. Couldn't.

"Good," Betty said firmly, but she didn't elaborate. Then she sighed. "I don't want to… Listen, the people who've told us these twins are yours aren't exactly the most trustworthy people on the planet."

That shocked him enough to look away from the kids to stare at Betty. "You don't think they're mine?"

She reached out and put a comforting hand on his arm. "It's not that. It's that I think there could be something more at play, and until you do a paternity test, you won't know for sure."

Garret looked back down at the babies, the boy trying to roll over while the girl played happily on her back, reaching for her brother.

Maggie and Cain.

Maybe they weren't his. Maybe they were bait. But regardless of biology, of what Savannah was using them for, they were two innocent lives.

And he'd do everything in his power to protect them. No matter what.


"So, what's next?" Betty asked gently. He seemed almost afraid to touch the children. He just kept watching them with that awed, wide-eyed look. This wasn't the same man who'd been angry this morning. The children had softened him in this moment.

But as much as she wanted to, she couldn't give him the space to be soft. That woman out there in the cabin somewhere wasn't anyone they could trust. They were… vulnerable, being in her cabin. They needed a plan. They needed North Star.

Betty walked over to the window and pulled back a curtain. "Shay should be here soon, I would think." Outside, the world was a bright white. But not just the white of snowdrifts—more was falling from the sky. Betty frowned. "It's snowing."

"It's more than snowing. It looks like a blizzard."

Dread pooled in Betty's stomach as she looked back at Garret. He was still crouched by the babies, but he was looking out the window.

"Maybe they got here before it hit," she said hopefully. But she'd spent enough years in South Dakota and Wyoming to know how fast weather could turn, and how dangerous it could be. But these were North Star operatives they were talking about. "They could be out there assessing the situation."

Garret slid her a disbelieving look, but didn't say anything to argue with her. "We'll be stuck here. Regardless of who's out there. No one can get off this mountain in a blizzard."

"Stuck here with Savannah."

Garret scowled. "She hasn't tried to kill us yet. I guess that's something."

"I don't think she's in the market to kill you. Me, on the other hand…" Betty knew she didn't have to say it, but she figured it was best just to lay it out there. Because Garret seemed clueless to *that* tension. "She thinks there's something going on between us."

Garret didn't look up from Cain, who had begun to whimper. The kids were probably due for a feeding.

"Even if there were, it wouldn't be her damn business," Garret said gruffly.

Betty's stomach turned over. "Rationally, but emotionally?" She knew *she* should be rational, but there was an underlying emotion. Especially standing here watching Garret hold his son.

Rationality didn't always win over emotion.

"She didn't love me." He shook his head. "She couldn't have loved me and done that."

Something bitter slid down Betty's throat. She swallowed against it, tried to keep her words devoid of the emotion that threatened to churn deep inside. "Does love to you mean self-sacrifice?"

"Yes."

"It doesn't to everyone."

He gave her a confused look, but she couldn't... She couldn't go there. Not here. Not with so much going on.

"I need to contact Shay somehow."

"I don't think Savannah's going to lend you her cell."

"It wouldn't work up here anyway. We need to find the landline, and we need to distract her enough so I can make the call. I don't want her knowing. I don't want... I don't trust her, either. She doesn't need to know about North Star."

Garret nodded. "Agreed."

"The babies are probably due to eat. So, we'll go back out there and see what we can find. Just try to keep an eye on her. I don't want to die at the hands of an unreasonably jealous ex of yours."

He looked at her, holding her gaze. Something in his expression had her heart tripping over itself.

"Define 'unreasonably,'" he said, something... *something* in his voice that made her shiver deep within.

Maggie began to cry in earnest, and Cain added his own voice to it. A cacophony of baby cries. "They need to eat," Betty said, surprised to find her voice sound... shaken. When she was never unsteady.

Garret finally broke from her gaze and looked down at Cain in his arms. "Hungry, huh?" he said softly. Then he moved for the door, opening it with his bad arm—

he was using that shoulder too much. He looked into the hallway, to the right and then the left, as if he was half-convinced he'd find a battalion of soldiers out there waiting for them.

Betty was a little close to being convinced of that herself. But Garret stepped into the hall and she followed, holding Maggie close to her chest. The babies *did* seem healthy, but Betty desperately wanted to make sure that was true.

If Savannah's grandparents had been taking care of the children they'd likely been tended to by a medical professional, but how long had Savannah had them? How much truth was there to the story the grandparents had actually *had* the children? Sure, they were legal guardians, but was there any proof the Lorens actually had the babies in their home for all these months?

Betty's stomach twisted in knots as she followed Garret down the hallway. Too many things didn't add up, and that was a clear sign she was in over her head. Garret should have a real North Star operative with him, not a doctor who knew how to change a diaper and sew up a gunshot wound and not much else.

Garret moved into the living room, but Savannah wasn't there. He frowned and turned back toward another doorway that Betty assumed would lead them to a kitchen. She followed Garret in silence.

When they stepped into the kitchen, Savannah was there.

But she wasn't alone, and Betty was suddenly aware of how much danger they were in.

## Chapter Eight

Garret didn't recognize the man who sat at the kitchen table with Savannah, but he immediately knew nothing good could come from a new person thrust into this situation.

A situation he'd dragged Betty into because he couldn't stop, think or accept help. Now she was in danger, and it was his fault and his fault alone.

He'd been going on emotion and reaction ever since he'd been shot. Like the cop part of himself he'd been honing for fifteen years had simply bled out of him. He'd expected healing to help him get back to his old self, but he hadn't had time to heal from the physical wound, and he wasn't sure time would ever heal this emotional one.

But this man, studying him and Betty with a cold, assessing stare, was the wake-up call he should have gotten a few days ago.

He couldn't go back. He couldn't change course. He couldn't wait around for the gunshot wound to heal or the betrayal to feel less soul crushing.

He had two babies and a woman to protect. It was time to find a way back to himself. The weight of fatherhood, of mistakes, he would deal with later. Right now he had to be the cop he'd been trained and had worked to be.

Garret looked from the man to where Savannah stood, behind the kitchen counter. She had a different expression on her face from all the fake niceties for him earlier or glares she'd sent Betty's way. Garret didn't know how to parse it, but it was clear she wasn't in charge anymore.

The man at the table was.

"They're hungry," Garret said, addressing Savannah and ignoring the man.

"I'm getting the bottles ready," she replied, though it was clear she was just standing there.

"I can make them if you'd like," Betty offered. She didn't look at either the man or Savannah. Her gaze was on Maggie in her arms. A smart tactic all in all.

"All right," Savannah said coolly. "Help yourself." She gestured to the corner of the counter, where there were bottles lined up next to other baby paraphernalia Garret didn't know anything about.

When all was said and done, he didn't want to take his children away from their mother, but if their mother was as dangerous as Savannah might be...

What would he do with two babies? By himself?

*Focus on now.* Now was the man in Savannah's kitchen. *Not* introducing himself. *Not* moving. Watching, cold and detached. As if he was planning something very bad.

Betty moved into the kitchen under Savannah's watchful eye, her nasty expression toward Betty never changing.

Garret couldn't believe it was jealousy. Not really. Savannah couldn't have done what she'd done *and* loved him. She couldn't fake her own death and then automatically think the woman with him was her *rival*.

It was ridiculous. But regardless of the motivation, Savannah clearly didn't like Betty or what she represented, which meant Garret had to keep an eye on that.

Garret watched Betty easily move around the kitchen, getting bottles, measuring out formula and warm water, all while holding Maggie in one arm. Like she had all the experience in the world with babies. Garret didn't know why his brain kept fixating on that.

He didn't know Betty in that way. He'd spent some time with her, enough to know her personality, to read her moods for as little as she gave away in her placid expressions and calm demeanor. But he didn't know a thing about her past.

"Finally, someone to take care of these kids," the man said, still studying Garret. The word *kids* sounding like a bad word when this man said it. "I haven't slept in weeks."

Weeks. Garret filed that away. How long had his children been here when they were supposed to be with their great-grandparents? When Savannah was allegedly hiding herself from her grandfather?

Her story didn't add up, and he knew she was using those children to keep him off balance. To keep him from asking the questions that needed to be asked.

But he didn't care about the questions or the answers. Let Betty's North Star take care of that. Once this blizzard was over, he'd take his children home. Everything else that came after that he wouldn't worry about. He had nothing to do with this, except somehow Savannah had once involved him in whatever this all was.

So he didn't care. He didn't *care* about anything aside from Cain and Maggie. His only goal was to get his babies safe and sound and *home*, and to make sure Betty got out of it without a scratch.

"So, Garret Averly, what can you tell me about North Star?"

Betty made a noise, but it was quickly covered up by a cough. Garret kept his gaze on the man. He didn't have a clue what he was after, but he knew instinctually to do whatever he could to keep Betty out of it. If he was asking Garret about North Star, that meant he didn't know Betty was a part of the group.

Garret would make sure to keep it that way. "I don't know what you're talking about."

The man's eyes narrowed. "Who are the folks who got your brother out of a jam?"

"Who wants to know?"

The corner of the guy's mouth curved. Slowly, he reached under the table and pulled out a gun. Again, Betty made a sound, but Garret kept his gaze steady on the barrel of the gun.

"Let's be clear. I'll ask the questions. You'll answer them."

"Or?" Garret returned.

The man's eyebrows rose. "Was the gun not clear enough? I'll shoot you. I'm not here for you. Or for the kids—they were a pawn to get you here, Garret Averly, upstanding small-town cop. I'll use all of you to get North Star right where I want them. That's the only thing I'm after."

Garret slowly moved his gaze to Savannah. Her expression was hard. "I'm telling you this isn't the way to do it. You should have waited," she said to the man in the chair.

"I got tired of waiting, *Savannah*," the man returned, waving the gun as if it was an extension of his arm. As if trying to prove how little he cared if it accidentally went off.

Garret held himself still as he filtered through his options. He could charge the man, but the table between them gave too much of an advantage to the guy with the gun. And…that was about the only option aside from wait and see.

This man knew about North Star. Down to the name—which Garret himself hadn't known until Betty had let it slip. Before that everyone he'd dealt with— Shay, Elsie, Mallory, even Nate—hadn't mentioned the name of their group.

Did North Star know someone knew about them? Was after them? Was that why they hadn't shown up yet?

In the end, it didn't matter. Getting Betty and the kids safe mattered. Which for now meant standing here and…dealing with this man. Keeping him from feeling the need to shoot any of them.

"Why don't we go feed them in their room?" Betty said gently into the silence. "You've made it clear you don't need us." She slid a look to the man, but mostly she kept her face averted.

So Betty understood it, too. He didn't know she was

with North Star, and they had to be careful to make sure he didn't find out.

"That's where you're wrong," he said, leaning his elbows on the table. "I need you. It just doesn't matter if you're dead or alive." He made another hand motion, this time with his empty hand. "Savannah, stick the woman with the babies in that room. Lock it from the outside."

"That I'll do gladly," Savannah said with a nasty grin. She sauntered up to Garret. "Hand him over."

Garret looked at her. "If you were trying to play me, you failed."

She rolled her eyes. "*Play* the noble Garret Averly? Surely that's impossible." She snorted. "Give me the baby." She held out her arms.

"I'd rather—"

"If you want them alive…" The man nodded, the gun pointing straight at Maggie and Betty. "You'll give the kid to Savannah. Now."

BETTY DIDN'T BREATHE. She had no idea what Garret would do. She had no idea what any of them were supposed to do. All she could think was she was not prepared. All those years she'd patched up North Star operatives and denied Shay's offers to train her in some way.

She should have taken her up on it. She should have learned how to be more than a healer. She'd always thought it went against her moral code. That it was inviting everything she'd escaped back to her doorstep.

But now she realized it was survival, and God, she'd been stupid to refuse to learn how to survive.

Garret carefully transferred Cain into Savannah's arms. His face was stone-cold fury, but he said nothing and held himself rigid. He needed his bandage changed. He probably needed some painkillers. He wasn't one hundred percent, and there was nothing she could do about it.

She wanted to cry, but she couldn't do that, either. She had to be strong. Maybe it wasn't so different than her work as a doctor. She had to be strong for her patients. Clear-eyed and calm in the face of disaster and emergency.

*Stay calm*, she ordered herself. *For Garret*. She looked down at the serious, wide-eyed baby in her arms. *And these babies*.

"Come on," Savannah said to Betty, and Betty didn't know what else to do but follow. That man would kill all four of them. If she wasn't reading things wrong, he'd *relish* killing all four of them.

But if that were true, wouldn't they already be dead?

She looked down at Maggie in her arms. She didn't know what kind of monster this man was, but the woman in front of her…

"Don't you care about your children?" Betty asked in a low hiss as they moved through the hallway. How could Savannah allow any kind of threat to her own offspring?

Savannah pointed into the kids' room. "Get in."

Betty listened, but she couldn't quiet the wave of fury she felt toward this woman putting her children in harm's way like this. She stepped into the room but then turned and scowled at Savannah. "Shame on you."

Savannah stalked across the room, put Cain down

in the crib. "Call me when your life is on the line, and we'll talk." She marched back to the door, then gave Betty a nasty smile. "Oh, wait, it is." Then she slammed the door shut.

Maggie jerked in Betty's arms and then the two babies began to wail in unison. "It's all right, sweetheart." She brought the girl to her chest and rested her cheek against the soft baby's. "We're going to make things all right," Betty crooned.

She moved over to the crib and reached inside to rest her hand on Cain's belly. A desperate need to protect these two innocent lives waved over her. "I'm going to do whatever I can to keep you safe. And so is your daddy."

*Daddy.* So many conflicting feelings. But this wasn't about her.

Maggie quieted first, nestling into Betty's arms as Betty fitted the bottle into her mouth. She looked around for a toy to occupy Cain until she could feed him his bottle.

They were expecting her to care for four-month-old twins locked in this room. Who needed food and love and space. Not just a crib.

Betty sat in the rocking chair. She had to breathe through the fear. Mostly for the little babies, who might not understand what was going on but might sense her disquiet and begin to cry.

She'd felt fear before. Been threatened before. Life was precarious, especially when you were involved with North Star. And all she'd dealt with before she'd gotten there.

But the man with the gun *knew* about North Star when no one was supposed to.

*He doesn't know you're North Star*, she reminded herself fiercely.

She had a leg up on him. As long as he didn't kill Garret. As long as…

"One step at a time," she whispered as Maggie sucked down her bottle. Once she'd finished it, Betty burped her and then set her in the crib and handed her a little rattle to play with. She fed Cain and studied the room.

It was utilitarian at best. Diapers and blankets and this rocking chair. A baby monitor and a few toys. But no decorations. No permanent evidence children belonged here.

It reminded Betty of when North Star had rescued some girls from a biker gang. They'd stayed in Betty's medical center while she'd checked them out, and Betty had rushed to find ways to make the children comfortable—but it had still been a medical center.

"I don't think you've been here that long," she whispered to Cain. She scooted the rocking chair closer to the crib so she could reach through the slats and stroke Maggie's arm. "But I'm not convinced you've been with your great-grandparents, either. I'm not convinced of much, actually."

Except that Shay would come. Or one of the North Star operatives would. Maybe the blizzard would slow them down, but someone would be here.

But were they walking into a trap?

## Chapter Nine

The man said nothing else. He sat. Savannah went behind the counter, then moved around and made a sandwich, of all things. She set it in front of the man, and he set his gun down to eat. Savannah took the seat next to him.

Garret didn't move, standing still as a statue, watching the man as he tried to formulate a plan. He was relieved Betty and the babies weren't in the same room with that gun anymore, but that didn't make things good. He didn't like the fact they were split up.

But they were in the same house. And while this man had a gun, he was one man. Savannah didn't seem to be armed, and as far as he could tell there wasn't anyone else waiting in the wings.

The man finished the sandwich, watching Garret the entire time. Garret easily held the man's gaze. He wasn't afraid of this man, and he wasn't about to act like he was. He ignored Savannah's presence completely.

"The blizzard messed up my plans, I'll admit," the man said after a while. "Sometimes, Mother Nature just doesn't cooperate." He wiped his mouth with the back of his hand. "We'll be waiting here a little longer than I'd planned. Honestly, I'd prefer to kill you, but Savannah had some good points about keeping you alive."

Garret wanted to look at Savannah's expression at hearing that, but the way the man's stare narrowed kept Garret's eyes meeting his. He wouldn't be jerked around by this guy, and he wouldn't give the guy what he expected.

"She was right about you, though." The man let out a low whistle. "Quite the cold, boring fish."

Garret wanted to laugh. As if either of their estimations of him would matter to or bother him. These *criminals*. Instead, he worked on being an even quieter, colder, more boring *fish*.

So far the man had given very little away—except that he wanted North Star to come after them—so Garret would give even less of himself. Though the big problem was that Savannah knew...everything.

He'd married her because he'd loved and trusted her. Even if she hadn't been pretending—which he found very hard to believe—whatever had once been was long gone.

*Does love to you mean self-sacrifice?*

He didn't know why Betty's words would come back to him in that moment. Why they would sit like a guilty weight on his heart. He wasn't in the wrong here. Wasn't that clear?

"Any sign of them?" the man asked.

"Not yet," Savannah said. "Just put him in another room. No one could make it through this blizzard. We've got time."

The man continued to study Garret. "We don't need him. He's better to us dead."

"Unless they want proof of life. Or an exchange. Come on, Cl—" At the man's sharp look, Savannah stopped herself. Garret assumed from saying the man's name.

"We have to keep him alive until we get to the next step. Then you get to do whatever you want."

The man drummed his fingers on the table. He pushed the now-empty plate toward Savannah. She dutifully took the plate and walked it over to the sink.

"All right. But not a room. Use the shed."

Savannah looked startled. "But…that's outside."

"We don't need him dead. We don't need him in good shape, either. I don't care if he gets hypothermia."

"No, I'm not worried about the cold," she said, eyebrows drawn together as if thinking hard. "I don't know if the shed would keep him. He's a cop. He's from here. He knows how to survive. You'll blame me if he escapes."

"Yes, I will." He lifted the gun again. He didn't point it at Savannah, but he didn't have to. "We've got the lady and the kids. North Star will still come." The man sized Garret up. "*Maybe* he comes in useful. I'll give you that. But not more useful than a woman and kids. I know who I'm dealing with."

"What if he escapes?" Savannah pressed.

The man shrugged negligently. "It's either keep him alive, and I blame you if he escapes, or he's dead." The man smiled at Savannah. "Pick your poison."

Savannah stared at the man. There was anger in her

eyes, but she didn't scowl at him like she had at Betty. She didn't talk back. "Do I get the gun?"

The man threw his head back and laughed, a long, loud, obnoxious bark. He scraped the chair back and got up. "You're a riot." He moved behind the counter, where there was a black duffel bag on the floor.

Garret watched as the man pawed around in it, but he couldn't see anything inside. The man pulled out a pair of handcuffs, and then what Garret assumed were some kind of ankle chains.

"Use these," he said, tossing them at Savannah. She struggled to catch all the clanging metal thrown at her. She frowned at them, but untangled everything and then walked over to Garret. She raised an eyebrow at him. "Going to make this hard?"

Garret considered his options. Allow her to chain him up and take him out to a shed—that even Savannah thought he'd be able to escape from—or what? Fight a man with a gun while his shoulder was injured?

He held out his hands to let her put the cuffs on him. She rolled her eyes. "Behind your back. I'm not going to make this *easy* on you, or did you not hear the part where my life depends on you staying put?"

Her life. Garret didn't know what to do about this. On the one hand, he didn't trust Savannah. What she was involved in. That her life was truly dependent on what he did. On the other hand, he wouldn't put anything past the man with the gun.

He put his hands behind his back and she cuffed him. A very strange sensation to be on this side of being cuffed. She put the ankle chains on as well, so he had to shuffle step to follow her—through the kitchen, out the back and into the frigid cold.

He still had his coat on from before. It was his only saving grace against the biting wind and snow.

He trudged behind her through the snow. There'd been some kind of path dug out of the previous snowfall, but the blizzard had dumped more inches into the gap. Savannah tromped through it all easily, but the ankle chains on him made it difficult.

He narrowly managed to catch himself before he fell, but it jerked his shoulder and he hissed out in pain.

Savannah looked over her shoulder at him. Studied him. "What's wrong with you?"

"Is this cold and these restrictions not enough for you?"

A shed came into view, but the snow was coming down so hard he hadn't seen it until they were basically standing in front of it.

This was all so surreal. He could only watch Savannah try to dig out the door to this small, rickety shed.

"What have you gotten yourself into, Savannah?"

She didn't answer. She kept scooping snow away from the door of the shed before pulling it open. "Look. I know you can probably get out of this. But I'm dead if you do."

"It doesn't have to be that way," Garret said. He didn't trust Savannah, or that man. He didn't trust anything that was happening. But he couldn't… He didn't want Savannah to *die* at the hands of that man. Pay for what she'd done? Sure. But not *die*.

"Yeah, it does," she returned. "So, you know, my

life's in your hands. Congratulations." She studied him, and he expected to find fear or fury in her gaze.

What made his stomach turn was how *resigned* she seemed. Like she had indeed gotten herself into something she couldn't get herself out of.

Which begged the question. Did he try to get her out of it?

BETTY HAD PLAYED with the twins, then gotten Cain back to sleep. Maggie remained quiet, but she wouldn't close her eyes. Betty had rocked, sung, jiggled. Now she had resorted to pacing the room, but the girl just stared at her with big brown eyes.

Were they Garret's eyes? Savannah's were blue. Of course, genes didn't work that straightforwardly, but…

She wanted these babies to be Garret's simply so he didn't have to go through another upheaval. So that whatever came from this he could just…

"Oh, hell," Betty muttered out loud. "I guess it doesn't matter until we get out of this, does it?" She stroked Maggie's cheek as she made another circle around the room. "You're a quiet soul, aren't you?"

For what felt like the hundredth time, Betty looked around the small, cramped room. There had to be a way to communicate with North Star. She couldn't escape through the windows and leave the babies here—though she had a sneaking suspicion there would be no way to get that window open anyway.

There was no way to escape. She had to get that possibility out of her head. Even if Shay or someone arrived, she wouldn't leave these children behind.

Betty went to the window and pulled the curtains

back. The swirling white was still coming down thick. She knew if Shay thought there was danger they'd press through the blizzard. They had the supplies and the know-how to survive this major weather event, but… If they didn't know she and Garret were in immediate danger, they might wait it out.

Even if they didn't, that man in the kitchen was waiting for them. He wanted North Star.

*Why?*

If she thought too much about that it practically paralyzed her. No one—*no one*—was supposed to know what North Star was. She'd slipped up and mentioned the name to Garret—something she still couldn't parse. But most people, even the people they worked to help, didn't know the name of their group or where or how to find them.

She dropped a kiss to Maggie's forehead, then carefully placed her in the crib with Cain's sleeping form.

She could try to sleep herself. It might be important depending on what would come after, but she knew even if she lay down and closed her eyes and used her usual calming techniques, she wouldn't sleep.

She returned to the window, looking at the world outside. A swirling mass of white, white and…

She squinted, practically pressing her nose to the glass in an effort to make out what that…*smudge* was. Cutting through the white. Two…figures. Two people. They moved across the yard, closer to her window, but clearly that wasn't the destination.

She could make out some kind of outbuilding a ways away in the direction they were walking.

As they got closer to the window on their path toward

the building, Betty could make out Garret and Savannah. Something sour twisted in her stomach, but she ignored it, focusing on what they were doing.

Garret's hands were behind his back and he walked awkwardly. Like he was… He was bound. Hand and ankle chains or something. They reached the building—some kind of shed from what Betty could see through the snow and from her vantage point inside.

After a brief pause during which he and Savannah clearly had some kind of conversation, he stepped into the shed.

Savannah closed the door and secured a padlock on it. She'd locked him inside that…small shed. In this blizzard? It was too cold. He was *injured*.

A hot wave of fury worked through her. How dare these people treat them like this? After everything Garret had already gone through—all things that had absolutely nothing to do with him. He hadn't asked to be drawn into this. Maybe Nate hadn't deserved what had happened to him, but at least he'd been *involved*. Not just a random brother thrust into the middle of it because he might have some sway or influence.

Betty's fingers curled into a fist and she thought about pounding on the glass. Yelling at Savannah that she was basically killing Garret by locking him in that shed—and did she really want that on her conscience?

She stopped before her fist actually hit glass. Maybe it was better if Savannah didn't know she'd seen. And maybe Savannah didn't have a conscience. Shouting at people rarely got you what you wanted. So she dropped her fist and purposefully uncurled her fingers. She had to be smart about this. Garret didn't deserve to be caught up, but neither did these children. She had to stop thinking like a doctor and a victim and start thinking like a North Star *operative*.

The doorknob to the room door rattled and Betty whirled around. She needed a weapon. She needed *something* she could use if given the chance. But the room was so empty. There had to be something. If she got the chance, she'd search every inch of the room instead of wasting time looking out the window.

The man from the kitchen stepped into the room. He studied her with those cold eyes and a colder smile. "I learned something very, *very* interesting about you, Betty Wagner."

Betty's entire body went to ice. How did he know her name? He shouldn't. Not first and last. Not...

"I didn't realize we were dealing with one of North Star's own. That changes things, Betty. It changes a *lot* of things."

## *Chapter Ten*

Damn, it was cold. Garret didn't just hear the wind whistling through the gaps in the wood, he felt the icy knives of the gusts on every inch of exposed skin. He had winter clothes on, the type that had allowed him to hike through the snow during the day.

But now they were in a blizzard, and night would fall, and he wasn't moving to keep his body warm. He was handcuffed and ankle-chained. They were all things he could deal with…if he could only decide what to do.

His first plan had been to escape. Immediately. This dinky shed certainly couldn't hold him, even with the gunshot wound in his shoulder and the handcuffs. It would be harder with his legs chained as he couldn't give the door a few swift kicks, but his good shoulder could just as easily work as a battering ram.

He'd even stood there, shoulder to the door, in a ready stance to run and use his body weight to splinter the wood.

But he hadn't been able to make himself do it.

*My life's in your hands.*

It wasn't just Savannah's words that stopped him.

It was the resignation in them. That she didn't have a choice. She wasn't trying to paint herself as the victim. She hadn't begged him to have pity on her or tried to use his former feelings for her against him. She had just said those words. Fully and totally sure this was her fate—and she had no choice in the matter.

He did, though. *He* had a choice, and he hadn't done anything wrong to get himself put in the position where some strange man might kill him. *Savannah* had, and that wasn't his fault or responsibility.

But how could he get the hell out of here *knowing* she'd likely end up dead? That *would* make it his fault.

He couldn't just worry about Savannah, and he could hardly prioritize the woman who'd clearly waded into her own mess. Betty and his kids were inside with that *man*. There was a blizzard making it difficult for help to arrive.

But no matter how much he went over these things, he just kept coming back to one simple fact.

Savannah's life was in his hands.

He didn't have it in him to walk away from that.

There had to be something he could do. Could he make it to that window where Betty and the kids were? And then do what in the midst of a blizzard?

He was tempted to run at the door—not to escape, but to jar his own circular thoughts. Instead, he walked in a circle, hoping to keep his body as warm as he possibly could as the wind howled outside.

He wasn't sure how long he did that, but after a while the door slowly began to open. Garret held himself, ready to fight if he had to. Was Savannah just checking to make sure he was still here? Was it the man from the kitchen?

Instead, a tall woman dressed all in black slid through the half-open door. She flicked on a flashlight, pointed at the ground but illuminating the dim interior of the shed.

"You picked a hell of a time to do a runner."

Garret knew Mallory from when North Star helped Nate prove he wasn't lying about the military corruption he'd found. Mallory was a field operative, and she knew how to handle herself.

But she didn't know what she was walking into, that was for sure.

"All right. You're going to follow me out," she began. "With that gunshot wound, I'm going to send you back to stay at camp. I'll handle getting Betty—"

"What do you guys know about what's going on in there?"

Mallory frowned. "Unarmed woman, armed man. Betty's locked in a room with the babies. I know you don't want to leave them behind, but we aren't equipped to get them out yet. We've got to tread carefully, but you're not in the physical shape to do it, man. So, you gotta go to the camp."

Garret shook his head. She knew more about the situation than he'd thought, but she didn't know everything. "I can't go with you. I have to stay here."

"You'd rather stay inside this shed and wait around for…what exactly?" Mallory demanded, and he could tell she was already counting down. She only had so much time to get him out of here. "You're not even in there with your kids. I don't think—"

"The man in there? He's after North Star. He's using me and the kids and Betty as bait. He thinks North Star is more interested in saving the women and children, and he's right and you guys should be. But he's after you. He has a plan and I don't know what it is."

Mallory's expression smoothed out. Her complete lack of reaction was its own response. That rattled her. "What do you mean he's after North Star? Where'd you hear that name?"

"He named the group specifically. Now, he didn't know Betty was part of North Star, but he did know that I was involved in something enough that he was waiting for me to use as some kind of bait for you guys."

Mallory rubbed her hands over her face. "I've got to tell Shay," she said, and though she kept her expression bland and focused, there was a higher note to her voice. Fear.

"You've got to get Betty and my kids out of there. I don't care if you take down the guy or sneak them out. I just care that they're safe. And I'll stay here if I have to. Just get them out."

"If that guy is here for North Star—"

"If my kids and your own doctor become collateral damage in this thing that's all about you guys and has *nothing* to do with me and my children, that guy in there will be the last thing you need to worry about."

Mallory heaved out a sigh and whirled away from him. "He named North Star? Specifically?" she reiterated. "Did he specify anyone within North Star?"

"No. And like I said, he didn't know Betty was one of you guys, but he does know the name of the group. And he's lying in wait."

Mallory swore. "Okay. Okay." She shook her head. "Okay. Stay here. Stay put. I've got to go wave Gabriel off. I'll relay this information to Shay and we'll move to get Betty and the kids out, but we have to come up with a new plan. If he knows our name, he could figure out Betty's connection at any point."

Garret hadn't even considered that. "It seems like he's alone. No computer equipment. He's not communicating with anyone."

"Did you search the house?"

Garret pulled a face. "No. No, I was busy meeting my kids. We didn't even know he was there until a few hours in."

Mallory nodded. "You can still come with me, Garret. What's them knowing you're gone going to do?"

He should tell her. Obviously, he should give all the information, but he couldn't bring himself to. "The element of surprise is always better, isn't it?"

"I don't know about always, but we'll go with it. I'll be back. Stay warm."

She slid out the way she'd come, closing the door again. Leaving Garret with only one option.

Wait.

THE MAN STOOD THERE, quiet as death. He didn't move. He didn't speak. He didn't even smirk. It was like he was waiting for her to confess her involvement with North Star.

He'd be waiting a long time. *Forever* in fact, because there was absolutely nothing he could do to her that would make her break her promises to North Star.

Luckily the babies were sleeping. Betty didn't know

how long that was going to last. It was impossible to guess when she didn't know what their normal schedule was. But for now they were asleep and unaware of what was going on around them.

So it was just Betty and the man. In a rather serious staring contest.

He was a fool if he thought he could break a doctor. She might not be able to fight or defend herself in the same way the operatives at North Star could, but she knew how to play every mental game in the book.

Time passed. Betty said nothing, didn't move. Eventually, the man sighed, breaking first, just like she knew he would.

"All right. You're going to be tight-lipped." He shrugged lazily and then stepped toward her.

Betty wanted to scramble away—her heart certainly scrambled—but she had watched North Star operatives long enough to know that she had to hold her ground. *Had* to. She kept her feet firmly planted and lifted her chin. She wouldn't move. She wouldn't flinch.

"Ah, there's the North Star operative in you." His mouth curved and Betty had to ignore *all* the alarm bells going off in her head. He was going to try to physically intimidate her—one way or another. She had to stand up to it. No matter what.

"Pretty soon your friends are going to know you're here. And they're going to know I have you."

"And who are you?" Betty returned, keeping her tone as calm as she could manage.

The man's smile widened, but he didn't respond at all. He stepped forward again until he was close enough to reach out. He touched her hair.

Betty recoiled despite herself.

He chuckled darkly. "If you think that's bad, just wait. Because the bad news for you is I don't want to eradicate North Star. I want to *hurt* them. I want them devastated, broken down. I want them *miserable*. Not dead. Not gone. *Broken*."

Betty didn't move and she didn't say anything.

"You have no idea what I know, Betty Wagner. No idea." He cupped her cheek—his hand large and warm and terrifying as it smoothed down her cheek and onto her neck. Where he squeezed gently. "But it doesn't take much to know how I could break you."

Betty was frozen with fear. Not just for herself, but for North Star. She didn't know how one man could take down the entirety of her group, but the fact he wanted to hurt them as much as end them struck fear into her heart.

Her friends. Who had become her family. No, she wouldn't be the weapon he used. She had to think back to the few self-defense moves Shay had insisted on teaching her. The man's hand was on her throat, but he wasn't restraining her in any other way. She needed to hit something vulnerable. Could she stomp his instep or knee his crotch before he squeezed too hard?

But before she could decide what action to take, and before he took any action himself, someone cleared their throat at the door. The man didn't look away from Betty. He kept the gentle pressure on her neck and his terrifying gaze on hers.

"You're going to want to come look at this," Savannah said, sounding mostly unbothered by what she'd walked in on.

The man looked back at Savannah standing in the doorway. Betty's heart was hammering in her chest but she used every last ounce of energy to remain upright, to *will* him to go with Savannah and leave the room. She would fight him off if she had to, but him leaving of his own accord was the far better option for the babies asleep in the room.

"Seriously. You want to look. Now," Savannah said, and there was a gravity to her voice even Betty believed. After all, it wasn't like Savannah was bound to save Betty from anything. Whatever was going on out there was important.

He'd come back. Betty knew he'd come back. But she'd be ready for it.

If only he'd leave with Savannah for now.

He stood there, hand still on Betty's neck, gaze on Savannah. For minutes. At least. Finally, he released Betty and turned away from her. "I suppose I have time. It's not like you're going anywhere." He walked over to the door, brushing past Savannah. "This better be good," he said, menacingly.

Savannah didn't follow him right away. She looked at Betty once, her gaze indecipherable.

"You could help us," Betty whispered, her throat tight with fear and fury. "Your own children. Why would you let them be caught up in this?"

Savannah said nothing. She simply walked away, presumably to follow the man. She closed the door on her way out and Betty just barely heard the *snick* of the lock over her raging heartbeat and breathing.

She had to channel the anger, diffuse the fear. She had to be ready. He'd be back and she had to be *ready*.

This time, she would have a plan. A weapon, somehow. She would fight. No more hoping for North Star to save her.

She was going to save them all.

## Chapter Eleven

Garret was well acquainted with frustration. He'd been a cop for fifteen years. He'd dealt with all manner of things that had crawled under his skin and never fully let go.

He'd dealt with domestic abuse he hadn't been able to do anything about. Addicts who never could escape the cycle no matter what help they were given. People who just didn't seem to have any kind of moral compass.

But standing here doing *nothing* was one of the most frustrating, painful things he'd ever had to do. He was *built* to act, to help, to do. It was why he'd stepped in and worked with North Star to help clear Nate's name. It wasn't in his nature to stand back and let someone else handle things.

But his hands were tied, and it felt like the story of his life right now. Betty had told him to give himself a break what felt like years ago but had been only a day ago and he didn't know *how*.

Except to focus on the center of all this. He was staying put in this little shed, freezing his butt off while his shoulder throbbed with pain, to keep Savannah alive.

Savannah. His ex-wife, who'd cheated on him. Kept his children from him. Then lured him to this place to be some kind of bait. Why would he protect the woman who'd done all that to him?

*At your core, you want to—maybe* have *to—do what's right.*

Betty's words. Because when all was said and done, she understood him somehow. Deeper than he expected to be understood by just about anyone.

She was in there, protecting his children, and he trusted her to do it. He trusted North Star to get them out. And he trusted himself to do what was right.

Even if it felt all wrong.

Time passed and Garret fought with himself to stay the course. When the door opened slightly again, another small crack that Mallory slipped through easily enough, Garret didn't know what to feel. He was cold, exhausted and in pain.

Mallory's grim expression didn't help that any.

"Shay wants the best approximation of a map you can draw," she said, holding out a pen and small notepad, of all things.

Garret made a gesture to remind her he didn't have his hands free to draw.

"Oh, right." Mallory slipped behind him and the cuffs fell off easily enough.

"Draw the whole place. Where Betty and the babies are. You're going to wear a comm unit—that's nonnegotiable," she added before Garret could argue. "Hide it however you like, but communication is key to getting everyone out of this safe and sound."

Garret took the pen and the pad while Mallory pulled out the comm unit. He wouldn't argue with her on that score. It would make him feel more involved, and it wasn't likely to get Savannah killed so it was a win-win.

"I'm a terrible drawer," Garret grumbled, trying to bring the layout of the cabin to the forefront of his mind.

"It doesn't have to be art, man. Just an idea of where they are and the ways in and out."

There was something in her voice. A tension that had Garret pausing. He narrowed his eyes at her. In a very un-Mallory-like manner, she had her hands jammed in her pockets.

"What aren't you telling me?"

She didn't flinch and her expression didn't change, but there was *something* about the way her posture straightened infinitesimally that proved to him he was right. She was keeping something important and *bad* from him.

"I don't know what you mean. We're still canvasing the area, getting a read on things, but the blizzard is making that slow going and hard to figure out an exact escape route. Especially with babies."

"What aren't you telling me, Mallory?" he repeated, this time putting some *firm cop* into his voice.

She heaved out a heavy sigh. "There's only one guy and Savannah as far as we can tell."

"Isn't that a good thing?"

"One guy thinks he can take down an elite secret group? There's something more to this. It's some kind of trap for us, Garret. And we have to be careful."

"While Betty is in the middle of it? In that house with that guy and—"

"Betty's one of ours. Don't act like we're not doing everything we can. Now, would you draw the house so I can get it back to Shay and we can start a game plan?"

Garret frowned, but he focused on drawing the best approximation of the cabin he could. Trying to orient the cabin to the shed, north and south, and every detail he could remember down to windows.

When he was done, he held it out to Mallory, but he didn't release it when Mallory tried to take it. He held on, holding Mallory in place if she wanted the map.

"What is it you aren't telling me?" he said. Cool, calm, intractable. Betty would be proud.

"You are one stubborn, annoying *cop*," Mallory said, sneering at him.

"Yes," Garret agreed.

Mallory blew out a breath. "It's just…"

"What?"

"I really shouldn't tell you," she muttered.

"I'm not part of your little group, Mallory. Shay can't reprimand me. Whatever you tell me is told in confidence and doesn't have to get back to her. But this is *fraught*. And it involves my kids. And Betty—and yes, I know, you guys care about Betty, but so do I."

Mallory studied him for a long time. "There's something she's not telling me."

"Betty?"

Mallory rolled her eyes.

"Shay?"

"Yeah, Shay. There's something she's not telling anyone. She knows something more than she's letting on. I can't get it out of her. All of this is bad," Mallory continued. "That's what I know. Now I have to take that map back to her so we can do everything in our power to get Betty out."

He let her have the map and then he secured the comm unit in his ear. "One step at a time. First? Get Betty and the babies out."

Mallory nodded. "Agreed. I'll be back."

She slipped out of the crack in the door, closing and locking it back up again. Leaving Garret cold and alone once more.

With nothing to do but listen.

And worry.


SAVANNAH LOREN WASN'T a good person. She knew that deep in her soul, and had very few regrets about the choices she'd made. She didn't mind that she'd conned Garret Averly into marrying her. She didn't mind committing murder, which she'd done more than once now.

She didn't mind doing the hard work as long as she was compensated, and if she was honest with herself, doing awful things gave her a thrill. It made her feel powerful and alive in a way she never had before.

She owed some of that to Cliff. She'd been hiding out, doing the odd job for her grandfather, but Cliff had sought her out. Told her what she needed to do, even before Grandfather had been arrested.

Get the kids back. Lure Garret to her hideout. Let him handle the rest. All for a *very* big payout. The drawback had been taking care of the kids. She was no mother, no caretaker. Their constant needs made her want to do things she knew no *good* person would want to do.

But for now, they were necessary pieces of the puzzle. Maybe when they were adults she'd take them under her wing, but she had no use for babies.

So, no, it wasn't using her children that had her stomach tied up in knots. It wasn't even knowing Cliff would knock her around if he didn't like what she'd pulled him out of that room for. She'd been knocked around before. She'd be knocked around again, no doubt.

What bothered Savannah was something she hadn't expected.

Walking in to tell Cliff about what she'd observed, she figured if he'd been doing something important she'd bow out and keep watching. Nothing big had happened yet.

But then she'd walked in and he'd had his hand on that woman's throat. Savannah had felt…*something* she couldn't quite name or understand. And she hadn't been able to let him…continue. She just couldn't.

That woman hadn't done anything. Savannah might not care whether she lived or died, but murder hadn't been what was in Cliff's eyes.

Savannah was having a hard time moving past it.

"This better be good," he said from behind her as she led him to the laundry room.

"Our quarry has had a visitor," she said, pointing to the window Cliff had spent some time crafting himself. From outside the cabin, you couldn't tell there were people inside looking out. "Twice now. Once I figured you were expecting and I wouldn't interrupt, but the second visit escalated things, don't you think?"

"Two visitors?" Cliff asked, ignoring her question as he peered out into the quickly falling dark.

Savannah shook her head. "One visitor. Two visits."

"A woman?"

"Yup."

Cliff grinned. "Excellent. It shouldn't be long now, then. Let me finish what I was doing, then we'll get set up."

"Shouldn't we get set up now?"

Cliff stared at her as if she were a particular kind of ridiculous. "I was in the middle of doing something important. Are you questioning me?"

Savannah should say no and let him do it. Have at the woman who Garret clearly had feelings for. Honestly, Garret could develop feelings for a tree stump. For a cop he sure had a soft heart.

But Savannah thought of the look on the woman's face when Cliff had put his hand around her neck. She had known. That Cliff didn't want to kill her. She had known and she'd been horrified.

She'd probably be horrified that Savannah didn't mind getting knocked around a bit or playing those games. No doubt the pretty little thing in there would be disgusted by the things Savannah enjoyed.

And still, Savannah didn't know how to let him go back in there.

"Yeah, I guess I am questioning you, Cliff."

BETTY HAD PUSHED the set of drawers in front of the door. It had taken some extra time because she had to be careful not to make a sound as she dragged it and shoved it across the carpet.

She knew it wouldn't stop the man from coming back in here, but it would give her time to know what was coming.

Next, she fashioned a weapon out of the curtain rod that she'd had to pull off the wall. It wasn't sharp or even particularly heavy metal, but it could do some damage with enough force in the right spot.

Then she collected every piece of clothing she could. Once the babies woke up, she would start dressing them. Layer upon layer.

She grabbed as many diapers and wipes as she could, shoving them into a fitted sheet she'd fashioned into a kind of bag. She'd tie it to her back. Holding both kids was going to be a difficulty, especially with the snow, but she'd do the best she could.

Somewhere out there, there was a North Star operative, or several, who'd be able to quickly get them to warmth and safety. Betty just had to be resilient and determined enough to get them that far.

Food would be a problem, for all of them, but she needed to be prepared to move. She needed to believe North Star would come tearing through that blizzard and get them out, and she needed to make that initial step to get the babies out of harm's way when harm inevitably came calling.

One of the babies began to fuss and she went over to the crib, picking up Cain before he woke up his sister. She crooned softly to him, changing his diaper and then slowly layering clothes on him. She made funny faces and he laughed and gurgled and Betty inwardly prayed, over and over again, this would work.

When Maggie began to stir, she repeated the process. She played a quick game of peekaboo, and then left the blanket over the babies for a brief moment. Quickly, she grabbed her makeshift weapon, prepared to break the window. Maybe they'd hear her.

But maybe they wouldn't.

She stood up and then had to swallow down a scream at the faces in the window.

Two faces. Two *familiar* faces. Betty blew out the breath she'd sucked in. Mallory and Gabriel. Two North Star operatives. They were saved. *Saved.*

Betty wanted to cry with relief, but she knew this wasn't over yet. They had to get out. Which was when she realized they were cutting the glass. A much quieter and more effective plan than breaking it.

She moved over to the babies and pulled the blankets off their faces. They both giggled in delight. "You're going to be safe with my friends. I promise," Betty whispered. Relief made her shaky, but they had a long way to go and she had to be strong.

She looked back at the window. Gabriel and Mallory were pulling a large square of the glass out. It was pitch-black, but the light from inside illuminated what they were doing.

"We're getting you and the kids out," Mallory said. She thrust her arms through the hole in the window. "Hand us each one, then climb out yourself. Okay?"

Betty nodded and bent down to pick up Maggie. She used the blanket they'd been playing peekaboo with to wrap around the infant. She moved over to the window. "This is Maggie," she said to Mallory, handing her through the large hole in the glass. Mal took the baby with ease and Betty went to grab Cain.

The clear, loud bang of a gunshot echoing through the house stopped her in her tracks.

Betty whirled to look at Mallory and Gabriel, but they both stood on the outside of the house, the light from inside illuminating their faces. They looked startled, but not shot or grim.

"Is that not you guys?"

They shook their heads. "We're just supposed to get you out. Not move on them. None of our guys out there are close enough to shoot, and even if they saw an opportunity to shoot it would be with a silencer and I really doubt they'd go that route," Gabriel said.

Which meant…

Betty swallowed and bent down to Cain. She wrapped him in the blanket he'd been lying on and then walked over to the window and transferred him into Gabriel's arms. "Take them. Get them out of here. I have to…stay."

"Betty—" Mallory began, but Betty cut her off.

"There are only two people in this house. I really doubt Savannah got a gun and shot the guy who's been… Look, whoever is shot, I might be able to save them."

"You can't be serious," Mallory returned, her voice taking on a surprising shrill note. Almost as if she was as panicked as Betty felt.

Which told Betty this wasn't a normal mission. Everything about this was off, but none of the details mattered to her.

She was a doctor. It was her job to help people if she could. Maybe she had no respect for Savannah, but she couldn't leave the woman to die. It wasn't right.

"Send someone back for me if you can, but no matter what? I have to do this. Now, go."

She didn't watch them to make sure they would go. She simply turned her back on them and strode to the door.

## Chapter Twelve

Garret heard the gunshot and stopped his pacing around the dark shed. His whole body seized in panic. *Who* had been shot?

There were too many terrible answers to that question. He could withstand a lot of inaction, but not this.

He moved for the door, ready to break it down, but it opened before he could get there himself.

It wasn't Mallory this time. Even in the dark he could tell a difference in height and body shape from the shadow. But before he could prepare to defend himself, a light clicked on.

It was Shay, a flashlight attached to her tactical vest. There was no stealth here. Just bursting in. "We're getting the kids out. Gabriel and Mallory have them both and are taking them to a helicopter waiting a ways away. Someone was shot inside that house and Betty stayed so she could help."

"Is she *insane*?"

"That was going to be my question for you. What's going on in there that would possess her to stay and help?"

"Hell if I know. What are you going to do about it?"

Shay heaved out a breath, as if she'd been running. And it had actually taken a toll. Garret wasn't sure he would have noticed it if Mallory hadn't been in here worried—about what Shay wasn't saying specifically.

But there was something…different about Shay from when he'd worked with her to help Nate. He couldn't go so far as to call it a wildness, or panic, but he figured it was as close as someone who was a tough veteran operative got to those states.

"Look, this is…big. Bigger than you think. So just… I can't go in there. I can't send my people in there."

Garret couldn't believe what he was hearing. "*Betty* is in there. She is one of your people."

"Yes, I know. Why do you think I'm here? I either send you in and hope it's enough, or I sentence everyone who works with or who has *ever* worked with North Star to a terrible death. That's a lot of people—a lot of people who've left and built lives that would be destroyed. More than you can imagine. This isn't my first choice. It's the only choice." She held out a gun for him to take.

Garret's mind whirled, but he took the outstretched gun.

"Got something to get these off?" he asked, pointing at his feet.

She bent down to cut off the shackles with a tool from her vest.

"It could have been Betty who was shot."

"It wasn't. Mallory and Gabriel were with her when the shot happened. It was in a different room than they were in or the ones we had eyes on, so no one knows who, but it wasn't Betty or the kids."

"Then it was Savannah."

Shay stood up. "Seems most likely. Unless she went against the guy."

Garret shook his head, testing out the weight of the gun and getting a feel for it. "She didn't have a gun. He did."

"Well, we haven't heard anything else, so he hasn't shot anyone else," Shay said.

*Yet* seemed to hang in the air between them. Garret looked at Shay. This was so different from how she'd been with Nate's problems. "What is this about?"

"Do you want me to explain while Betty is in there with someone who apparently has no qualms about shooting people?"

She had a point, but that didn't make Garret any more comfortable.

"You've got a comm unit," Shay said, pointing to his ear, where the one Mallory had given him was placed. "We've got eyes on every vantage point we can. Granted, a lot of places in the house we can't get a visual, but we've also got a camera for you. I'm going to attach it to your coat collar, so you need to keep the coat on. It'll give you eyes from the back. If we see anything coming for you, we can warn you."

"And you can get an ID on the guy. Unless you already know who he is?"

"I don't, but I know who he works for. You can't be too careful, Garret. If you thought what Nate went up against was big, you don't have a clue what this group can do. Take him down someway and then get you and Betty out of there."

"What about Savannah?"

Shay looked truly shocked. "What *about* Savannah?"

"She's been shot."

"She's one of *them*."

"Is she?"

"Uh, yeah. She lured you here, Garret. You don't honestly think you just outsmarted her, do you?"

He didn't like that line of thinking. So he focused on all the details Shay had given him. "So you've got the place surrounded, but you can't go in."

"This is bigger than just that guy in there, Garret. The minute I send my team in, we're surrounded."

Garret's eyebrows rose. "What does *that* mean? Are you surrounded right now?"

"In a fashion. Listen. You get in. If you can take the guy down without killing him, great. If you have to kill him to keep you and Betty safe—that's your call."

"Okay, and what happens when I do either of those two things?"

"You get out. As quickly as possible. You and Betty just start walking north. Carefully, though. Find one of us. We'll be scattered throughout. Betty knows our code. Then we can all get out of here."

It didn't make sense to him, but he didn't have time for sense. He didn't have time for anything, except… "Promise me my kids are safe."

Shay nodded. "They'll get on that helicopter any minute now. They'll be taken to an isolated ranch with my most trusted man. One of our medical staff—trained by Betty herself—is on the way there now. So they'll be safe and in good hands."

Garret inhaled. Then he nodded. "All right. Let's move."

"I'm counting on you to bring her out, Garret," Shay said, something almost like a tremor in her voice. "Don't disappoint me."

"I won't." He wouldn't be able to live with himself if he didn't get Betty out of this mess.

He slipped out of the shed into the frigid night. The wind wasn't howling and he didn't feel snow slapping him in the face, so the blizzard must have passed.

He looked across the yard to the warm lights of the cabin. A cozy picture. Like a postcard.

An utter lie.

BETTY CREPT THROUGH the hallway. She heard low tones—the man speaking, a seemingly one-sided conversation. Was he on the phone?

It was the first time she'd really given thought to what was beyond that man. Who did he work for? He didn't sincerely think he alone would take down North Star? Of course not. There was something…bigger than him.

Nausea churned in her stomach, but there was nothing she could do with that terrifying reality. She could only deal with the here and now. Find Savannah. Make sure she was okay. Then if Betty had to make a run for it, she would.

And hope like hell North Star was somewhere out there to help her.

Betty moved forward through the hall listening to

his voice. Quiet and indistinguishable enough that it sounded like he was in the kitchen or maybe even the room beyond the kitchen.

She didn't know where the gunshot had come from—back there? Living room? It had been too loud and sudden to get a sense of direction. So she could only search the house trying to find Savannah and hoping she was fine. First, she poked her head into the kitchen. No one. The man was definitely in the room just beyond—some kind of utility room Betty had caught a glimpse of when she'd been making the twins' bottles earlier.

Savannah could be in there with him. She could also be dead, and all of this pointless. Betty should have gone with Mal and Gabriel and the babies, but...

She shook her head. She had to be certain Savannah didn't need medical attention. She retraced her steps and tiptoed into the living room, where she and Garret had first talked to Savannah.

And there was Savannah in the dark room, a weak slash of light from the kitchen illuminating her. Instead of standing looking angry and accusatory toward Betty, she lay on the floor. Still and pale. She was somewhat propped up against the couch and though she didn't move, her eyes did. Landing on Betty.

She held her side. Blood seeping through her fingers. Betty hurried over. She didn't have her tools, and she would need them to fully help Savannah, but she could do some basic bandaging that would hopefully negate the blood loss.

Betty looked around for something she could use as a makeshift bandage. There was a quilt hung over the back of the couch, but it would be too thick to tear. Betty shrugged out of her coat and ripped at the hem of her own shirt, tearing off strips until there wasn't much shirt left. She shrugged her coat back on and began to work.

"If he comes in here and sees you mopping me up, he's going to shoot you, too," Savannah said. She was pale, maybe in shock. "Or worse," she added.

"Then he'll shoot me, too, or worse," Betty returned. There weren't options here. She'd taken an oath to help people in medical need and Savannah was in serious medical need. If it ended up being detrimental to Betty's own life…well, that was the risk she was taking.

Betty scanned the room again. Regardless of the man, if she couldn't get Savannah out of here sooner rather than later, or at least to some medical tools, the young woman wouldn't make it.

For real this time.

But Betty couldn't think of it that way. She had to think of what she *could* do, not what she couldn't.

Betty put pressure on the wound, using her strips of shirt and Savannah's own. It needed to be cleaned out and stitched up, and that was only if the bullet had cleanly passed through her side.

"Can you move at all?"

"Yeah, I think I'll get up and do a tap dance."

"Roll onto your right side as much as you can," Betty ordered. If Savannah could make jokes, that was at least some kind of positive sign.

"Look, I don't know what you think you're doing, but you might as well let it alone."

"I'm a doctor, Savannah. I'm not going to let it alone. Now, roll onto your right side."

Savannah moved, biting her lip. She didn't groan, though Betty could tell it was a hard-won thing.

"You're like…a real doctor?" she asked, her voice strained with pain.

"Yes. A real doctor," Betty said, inspecting Savannah's back. It appeared the bullet had passed through, but the wound was nasty. Close range for sure, though clearly aimed somewhere that wouldn't kill her immediately.

Betty thought back to what the man had said to her in the room with the babies. This wasn't about killing. It was about ruining people. Causing pain. Sympathy washed over her for Savannah, even if she had been on the man's side.

"There's not much I can do for you without some tools, but I can stop the bleeding as much as possible until we have more options." She pressed against the wound, wrapping the strips of her shirt around Savannah's body and then tying them as tightly as she could.

"We don't have any options." Savannah's body slumped.

Alarmed, Betty checked her pulse. Not great, but she was still conscious. Just defeated.

Betty couldn't allow herself to become the same. "There are always options, Savannah. Unless you give up."

"He shot me. I don't even know why I stood up to him. I knew he would shoot me. I knew he didn't care. I don't know what possessed me."

"What possessed you to do what?"

"I stopped him from going back after you. I don't

even care about you. I'd have killed you myself if he'd asked."

Betty stopped what she was doing for a moment. Very rarely in the course of trying to help someone was she caught completely off guard, but... "You were trying to save me?"

"I wasn't *trying* to. I was just... I don't know. Like I said, I don't care about you. I'd kill you myself given the chance. I would," she insisted, as if that was the part Betty didn't believe.

But the man hadn't been interested in *killing* Betty. At least not in that moment. Maybe Savannah had found her line in the sand, even if murder wasn't it. Betty focused back on the bleeding. "Sometimes it isn't about care. It's about doing the right thing."

Savannah snorted, then winced when the move clearly hurt her. "No wonder you're with Garret. Goody-goodies stick together. They die together, too."

Betty didn't bother to correct Savannah. It didn't matter, and it wasn't the point. Even if *together* settled strangely in her stomach. "I'm not the one with the gunshot wound."

"You will be. Soon enough. Or worse."

*Or worse.* Savannah kept saying that, but Betty couldn't think about it. She couldn't think about all the possible terrible outcomes. She had to believe that something would come along to help them, save them.

And if it didn't, she'd gotten those babies out of here. She'd done the most important thing. The rest would take care of itself.

Betty heard a sound from behind her. She froze, a cold, icy dread settling in her gut. She slowly looked over her shoulder at the opening to the kitchen, but didn't see anyone. She turned and searched for where the creaking sound had come from.

The front door. It was just barely ajar, moving farther and farther open, but she couldn't see who was behind it in the dark.

Until the barrel of a gun slid through the opening into the light.

## Chapter Thirteen

Garret kept low and crept inside the cabin. He listened for evidence that anyone was in this room with him. He heard the rustle of movement and slowly, carefully crept toward it.

He doubted it was the man since he'd likely shoot first and ask questions later. But he didn't know if it would be Betty or Savannah. Shay had given him a flashlight and a few other tactical tools attached to the vest she'd made him wear.

He got close enough to where he thought the rustling sound had come from and he flipped the penlight on. The tiny beam illuminated a leg clad in jeans. A woman's leg. Before he could speak he felt a sharp, painful whack against his shin.

He hissed out a breath, trying not to react loud enough it might attract the attention of the man, but another sharp rap followed quickly.

"Would you stop?" Garret muttered.

"Garret?" Betty's voice whispered, surprise tinging the volume of her whisper.

"Yes. Come on. We have to get you out of here ASAP."

"No, listen. Savannah's been shot. You need to get her out of here. She needs medical attention. Get her to a hospital and she might live."

"And leave you here?"

"Just for the time being. Shay—"

"Shay sent me in. She said she can't send her team in. I have to get you both out and take that guy down if I can."

"Jesus, Garret, are you out of your mind?" Savannah said, and her voice was half whisper, half groan.

"She needs a hospital," Betty said, stubbornly in his estimation. They had to get the heck out of here before they could worry about hospitals. They could all three get out…but if Savannah was compromised, they wouldn't be able to move fast enough.

If Savannah could walk well enough, Betty could get her to North Star and a hospital. And Garret could stay and stop the guy from following them. He could give them the time they needed to escape.

Then, whatever happened…happened.

"Okay," Garret agreed, crouching down so he could be eye level with Betty. "You'll get her out of here. Out the door, go north. Listen for a North Star signal. There are other people out there, so you have to be careful. I'll stay here and make sure no one follows."

"Garret, absolutely not," she said firmly, that doctor tone that brooked no argument.

Except there was an argument. There was only one way to make sure Betty had the best chance to escape and get Savannah to a hospital.

He took Betty's hand in his. She would argue, and they didn't have time for it. He had to get through to her. He looked right at her in what little light they had. "You have to do it, Bet." He squeezed her hand. "I have to stay."

She was shaking her head before he even got out the words. "You're injured. You can't fight like he can when you're injured."

"I'm a cop."

"He will kill you."

"Or I'll kill him. Either way, you'll all be safe."

"Garret, your babies need you. This is a suicide mission. We all go and—"

"And he follows. Or someone out there gets us. The longer I can give you guys a head start, the better chance you have of getting Savannah out of here." Which meant they had to stop arguing and start moving. "Savannah, can you walk?"

But Betty didn't let her answer. "I know you think you have to sacrifice yourself for everyone else but, Garret, you are a father now. You can't do that to them. Trust me—"

"Regardless of how bad a job she's done, Savannah is their mother. And you're the person who saved them. It's not about sacrificing myself. It's about what I could live with." He took her face between his hands, needing her to understand this. Needing…something he didn't have the time to untangle. Her face was soft, the set of her jaw stubborn.

He'd figure out why that swept through him later. After. "Go on, Bet. You can help her more than I can, and I can take care of this guy more than you can. It's the right thing to do."

She looked at him, and even in the dim light he could

see the tears sparkling in her eyes. They didn't fall onto her cheeks. She blinked them away and he covered her hands with his.

"All right," she said, and even whispering her voice came out strained. "I'll get her to someone who can get her to a hospital, but that doesn't mean I'm leaving you behind."

"Betty—"

She shook her head. He might have argued with her some more as they helped Savannah to her feet, but the low murmurings from the other room had gone silent. There was no time to argue. Garret just had to trust that North Star would keep Betty from doing something foolish.

Garret helped Savannah stay upright while Betty slid her arm around Savannah's waist. Once they were situated, he moved to the door and opened it only as far as they'd need to slide out of it.

Even as dim as the lighting was, he could tell Savannah was not in good shape. The frigid, snowy landscape outside wouldn't help any. But it was her only shot at survival, even if it was a small shot.

Garret didn't know how to feel about any of it, but luckily he didn't have time to feel. Once they were out the door, he spoke to them as quietly as possible, repeating the instructions Shay had given him. "Go straight. That's north. Keep moving north as quietly as possible. One of the North Star operatives will signal to you as soon as they can. They'll lead you after that. Just go north until someone from North Star finds you. Here—"

"I will not take your gun. It's your only chance to survive," Betty said firmly.

There was no time to argue. They had to get going. So he simply nodded and waited for them to clear the doorway. He didn't say goodbye. He didn't wish them luck. There was nothing to say or wish.

His only job was to give them time.

He closed the door as silently as possible and switched off the flashlight so he was plunged into darkness.

And the unknown.

BETTY WAS CLOSER to tears than she'd been this whole time. It felt wrong to leave Garret behind, but Savannah wouldn't survive if they didn't start moving. As it was, she could barely walk and Betty was carrying the weight of both of them through the snowy dark.

Garret had told her to move north. Carefully. He'd warned her there might be more men after them out here. But her instructions were to find a North Star operative.

"This is ludicrous," Savannah said. Her words were starting to slur and each step was more sluggish than the last. Betty urged her on nonetheless. Giving up wasn't an option. Garret was putting himself in harm's way to get Savannah to the hospital, so Betty was damn well going to get her to the hospital.

"Maybe it is," Betty said, clenching her teeth to keep them from chattering. "But what's the alternative?" she asked. She wanted to keep Savannah arguing, talking. Even though noise was a risk, the more Savannah moved and spoke, the better chance she'd stay conscious.

Savannah didn't respond, though. She was shivering. Betty couldn't give her the coat she was wearing because she'd ripped up her shirt underneath. She kept Savannah wrapped close to her as they took excruciatingly slow steps forward.

*North. Move north.*

Why was it taking so long? She knew they hadn't gotten far but surely a North Star operative could meet them now.

God, the air was so cold, and the snow was getting into her boots. She wasn't dressed for this. Savannah wasn't going to survive this.

*No.*

She would not let the negative thoughts win. Not when Garret was risking himself so they could get to safety. She began to hum quietly under her breath. It was a painful reminder of childhood, of her father. He'd always hum "Battle Hymn of the Republic" when things were bleak.

Toward the end, things had always been bleak. He hadn't made it out of all the complicated bad choices he'd made. All to save her.

To *save* her.

Now here she was. Saving others. He'd sacrificed for her and she'd let him.

Garret was doing the same thing. Risking himself for others—while his babies might never know him. All because he'd had to do the right thing.

Maybe it was different than her father—after all, the bad Dad had saved her from was of his own making—but it felt too much the same. Kids left without a dad all because he'd been intent on saving someone else.

The whole thing made her sick to her stomach.

"He's saving you, not me, you know," Savannah said, her voice weak and her weight getting heavier and heavier as Betty struggled to support her and take sure steps in the deep snow.

"What?" Betty had been so lost in her past she couldn't fully understand what Savannah was trying to say.

"This is for *you*. Not me."

"He could have left you behind."

"Not Garret." She shook her head. "I never did understand this do-gooder thing. I guess you've got it, too. What the hell are you doing trying to save me?"

"You tried to save me."

"Biggest mistake of my life," Savannah muttered.

"Not yet it wasn't," Betty replied. Her father was long dead, but *she* was alive. *She* had the chance to save Savannah. And Garret. Somehow. Someway.

SAVANNAH WONDERED IF any of this was worth it. Why not just lie down and *die*?

She didn't believe there was anything after death. If she believed that, she'd be judged for what she'd done, and she wouldn't have been able to murder the people she had.

Death was death. The end. All that mattered was life, and hers was draining out of her. Why would she fight that? She'd known that this was a possible eventuality every step she'd made for the past three years.

She'd made the decision to fall into danger and the moral low ground. Because it made her feel good. Alive. You could only do that if you had a healthy understanding of your own mortality—at least, Savannah thought so. What was the thrill of risking your life if you didn't think you might not come out the other side?

But that had been a hypothetical end. Now it was pain and a bleakness she both wanted to fight and give in to. Giving in to the bleak would be easy, and hadn't she always preferred an easy way out?

But this woman, a stranger, a woman who Savannah *hated* and would have killed if given the chance, was determined that she survive. Had even risked herself, and now the guy she was clearly in love with.

Garret.

Savannah's chest hurt. Not where she'd been shot deep in her side, but right in the center, where her lungs struggled to keep working.

She'd been disdainful of Garret's good-guy nature. How easy it had been to trick him into falling in love with her. Sure, the guy was hot and good enough in bed it wasn't such a hardship. She'd enjoyed the lies. Every night she went to bed satisfied she was *winning*.

She'd been glad when she'd been able to plant the cheating story. Less thrilled about the whole accidentally getting knocked up thing, but when she'd been convinced those kids could be pawns in the wider destruction, she'd enjoyed being a part of it. She'd let go of the bitterness over that.

Mostly. She *had* almost died giving birth to those two, and she couldn't say it was worth it. But they sure had been bait enough to make Garret easy pickings. That made North Star accessible.

Savannah didn't care much about North Star. That was her boss's deal. She just liked the big payout.

*And now you're going to die instead. All because you couldn't just let things go.*

"Just leave me here to di—"

Betty stopped walking and Savannah almost thought she was going to listen. Betty had finally reached her breaking point and was going to let Savannah lie in the snow and die.

Savannah was shocked to find a bolt of fear pass through her. When she was so sure she wasn't afraid to die. But suddenly…

Someone appeared before them, a small, narrow beam of light illuminating the snowy space between them—but not the figure. Just a black shadow.

"She needs a hospital. ASAP," Betty said.

"Got it," the shadow's voice said, coming for Savannah. She thought of fighting off the shadow, but she was lifted off her feet before she could even move her arms.

Things weren't making sense. Savannah's head was spinning. She was laid down on something and people were talking in low tones. She suddenly, desperately, wanted Betty's arm around her because that had felt solid. Real.

*Get a grip, Savannah.*

"Get in the vehicle, Betty," a man's voice said firmly. "I'll get us to the helicopter ASAP."

"No, I can't. You go, Connor. Get her to the hospital."

"Where the hell are you going to go?"

Savannah frowned at the conversation. They didn't make sense, but someone was already poking and prodding her, and she didn't have the energy to fight them off. A gray cloud was hazing the edges of her vision.

*I can't leave Garret behind like that.*

The words echoed around in Savannah's head. *She* could leave Garret behind. Easily. The guy could get himself shot for all she cared. This woman who'd saved her life, too. She'd watch them all die in a fiery explosion. She didn't care.

She *didn't*. But the more she tried to convince herself she didn't, the more she thought of what all this was. How easily Garret and Betty *would* be destroyed. They had no idea what they were up against. No idea the danger they'd planted themselves in.

They were clueless.

She should be glad. All that evil she'd helped build. It should thrill her to see it coming to fruition.

Her world was going grayer and grayer, and she didn't want to hold on. She wanted to succumb to the cloud. To leave all this behind. But before she did, she uttered the only word she could think of.

A word that might save Garret and Betty.

Or not.

"Vianni."

## Chapter Fourteen

Garret hadn't moved. As far as he was concerned, the longer he could avoid confrontation and make sure the man didn't catch on to the disappearance of Savannah and Betty, the more chance they had of getting out of here.

So he simply stood there in the dark, breathing evenly, and trying not to think about the throbbing in his shoulder. Waiting.

Betty and Savannah should be in the hands of North Star, safely. They wouldn't let Betty come back for him. He knew that. This was the kind of waiting he'd been trained to do. The kind of waiting that made him a good cop. He could wait for as long as it took.

Every second gave Betty and Savannah a chance to escape. Survive.

He heard movement deep in the cabin, but still no sign that the man had figured out the two women were missing. The light in the hallway flipped on and Garret held himself still, leaning against the front door, gun at the ready.

The man didn't even glance into the living room— presumably where he'd left Savannah to die. Slowly. Painfully. God knew the woman didn't deserve Garret's pity, after everything she'd done to him. But leaving someone to die that way… It was wrong. Period.

Garret curled his free hand into a fist. He couldn't let his anger get the better of him. So he centered it there in his knuckles. In the tension in his forearm. He carefully, loosely, adjusted his grip on the gun in his other hand so that it was ready.

Tense on one side, relaxed on the other. Ready for whatever came. Whatever he'd have to do to keep Betty safe.

Garret heard the muttered curse from deep in the house, then frantic movement as lights flipped on. Doors banged, more cursing. Still, Garret stayed exactly where he was. Poised. Ready.

Even if the man came charging in here, he wouldn't expect Garret. He had the upper hand.

That thought left Garret with an odd…discordant feeling inside of him. Like something was wrong. This overcomplicated plan, and it was going to end rather easily, all in all. When, really, Garret and Betty could have been killed or tortured. Quickly. Without all the locking into rooms and whatnot.

Garret inhaled slowly, carefully, and exhaled in the same manner. Once the immediate danger was over they could go over that, figure out the motives and if there was something more to all of this than it seemed on the surface.

But for right now his only objective was to eliminate the threat of this man in whatever way he could.

The man's breathing and under-breath swearing was

getting closer and with next to no warning the light in the living room flashed on.

Garret didn't flinch against it. He simply assessed the situation: man, eyes wild and fury turning his face red, with a too-tight grip on his gun, ready to shoot and cause whatever harm he could.

So Garret shot first. Before the man even registered him standing there. He aimed for a leg and when the man fell forward on a wail of pain, Garret was certain he'd hit exactly where he'd wanted to—debilitating the man without fatally wounding him, as long as they got him medical attention.

The gun fell out of the man's hand as he crashed to the ground and Garret lunged for it. He got it easily, kicking it toward the door. He had to paw around at the tactical vest to find something he could tie up the man with.

At the moment, the man was too busy holding his leg and groaning in pain. But it wouldn't take long for him to gather his wits and try to fight.

In one of the pockets of his vest, Garret finally found zip ties. He grabbed the man's arm and pulled it behind his back. The man finally began to fight back, shouting vicious curses, but his injury severely limited his mobility.

Once Garret had zip-tied his arms and legs, he dragged him over to where he could prop him up against the wall. He pulled some gauze out of one of the other tactical pockets and tied it around where the man's leg bled.

It hardly helped stop the bleeding, but it slowed the

flow. He got to his feet and studied the man. "Got him," he said into his comm unit.

The man looked up at him and laughed. "Yeah, buddy. You win." He continued to laugh, as if this was all some farce.

Garret had dealt with a lot of different criminals. Even some like this—sort of accepting of their fate, as if they'd always known this was exactly where they'd end up. But something about the *you win* made Garret immediately uncomfortable and unsure.

"Status?" Shay barked in his ear.

Garret took a step away from the man on the floor, then another. He looked away, not wanting the man to read anything into his expression. "He's shot in the leg," Garret said in low tones. "Tied up. Everything good out there?"

"Affirmative. Just leave him as is and meet me out here."

Come out there? That wasn't right. He lowered his voice so hopefully the man couldn't hear. "Don't you want to do a sweep? Come in and—"

"We will. Later. Come out, Garret. We'll get you home and we'll take care of everything else."

That was all wrong. Sure, Garret was injured, and maybe he wasn't part of North Star, but he'd done a mission with them before. It hadn't gone like this. Shay hadn't seemed so...secretive.

But this was it. They'd all gotten out and the man trying to take down North Star was incapacitated. Maybe Shay was worried about more men out there and wanted to clear the area ASAP.

"All right," Garret agreed, though none of this felt settled. But what else was there to do? They'd taken down the ringleader. Clearly Shay had eyes out there in the woods. They'd gotten the kids and Betty and Savannah out.

Whatever North Star had to do with this guy, they would do, and it had absolutely nothing to do with him. His part in it was finally over. He could go back to his real life because his involvement in *this* was over. Fully.

But why didn't it feel like that yet?

BETTY GLARED AT Connor Lindstrom. He hadn't been with North Star that long, but when she'd been insistent on getting back to Garret, he'd simply scooped her up, deposited her inside his Jeep and cuffed her to the door so she quite literally couldn't get out.

"Sorry, Shay's orders," he said, seeming not at all remorseful. He'd bundled Savannah into the back seat, making her as comfortable as possible while Betty tried to twist her hand out of the cuff, even though she knew it would be impossible.

Connor slid into the driver's seat. He reached over and buckled Betty's seat belt for her. He said nothing, just started driving.

"This is ludicrous. You should uncuff me so I can help her."

"You bound the wound. I don't have supplies, so that's about all you can do," Connor replied, driving through the snow and trees with ease despite the fact he didn't have headlights on in the faint light of pre-dawn. "Shay knew you'd try to make a break for it, but the team has Garret covered. You need to worry about getting you out of this safe and sound."

Betty didn't stop frowning, even if it was hard to argue with his logic. "Is someone else really still out there?" Betty asked, worry filtering through the outrage.

"Shay seems to think so. But we've got all hands on deck. I'll get you and her to a hospital," Connor said, nodding back toward Savannah. "The team will get Garret out of there. You know how this goes."

Yes, Betty knew how this went, but she didn't like it. Not with Garret back there waiting on a man who was capable of…anything. And if that man had more men out here in the woods…

Didn't that mean they were *all* in so much more danger than they were anticipating?

No, Connor was purposefully playing it down. So he could get her out of here with minimal argument. But she couldn't just…leave. Savannah needed a hospital, where she'd have better help than Betty could give her here. So Betty didn't need to go along.

"I am not getting on that helicopter. I know you're stronger and bigger and better at fighting than me, but I will fight dirty and you won't."

Connor's eyebrows rose, though he didn't take his eyes off the path in front of him. "Won't I?"

"Sabrina wouldn't love you if you would."

Connor's expression and ramrod-straight posture didn't change, but he grunted. As he often did when Sabrina was mentioned. She was the reason he'd even joined North Star, after they'd worked on a mission together. Sabrina was still recovering from her injuries from that mission, but Connor had started working with North Star as her replacement until she was back in fighting shape.

"Sabrina would let me go," Betty said, pressing the moment and her advantage.

Connor let out a sharp laugh. In another circumstance, Betty might have enjoyed it. He wasn't a man who laughed a lot.

"The hell she would," he said firmly. "She'd be rougher and meaner about bundling you up onto that helicopter, too."

Betty opened her mouth to argue, but Connor shook his head. "Look, I get it. She'd also do what you want to do in your position. So would I. It's not that we don't understand, Betty. It's just that we're handling it, the way we were trained. You were trained to help people like her. Not fight."

"What if he—*someone*—gets hurt?" Betty demanded. "I should be there to do what I'm trained for."

"I'm sure Shay has medics on the ground."

"Operatives who can field dress a wound are not the same as *medics*."

"Be that as it may—"

"You will not 'be that as it may' me, Connor. I have been with North Star far longer than you."

Connor pulled to a stop in a big clearing where a helicopter sat. She frowned. There couldn't be that many men surrounding the cabin if Connor could get in and out in the chopper without detection. "The babies are at headquarters?"

"Safe and sound," Connor agreed. "Now, let's…" He

trailed off and held up a hand. Betty could hear the faint buzz of someone talking in his comm unit.

"Lindstrom." He paused. Listened. "Got it. Will do." He turned to face Betty in the Jeep. "Garret's out."

"What?"

"He took down the guy. He's good to go. Shay's sending him back to headquarters with one of the team. We'll drop off Savannah, and then get you to headquarters as well."

"So it's over?"

"Seems that way."

Betty blinked, then eyed the helicopter suspiciously. This was all a little too easy. "You're not lying to me to get me on that helicopter, are you?"

He pulled the comm unit out of his ear. "Talk to Shay yourself. I'm going to get Savannah loaded."

Betty held the comm unit to her ear as Connor got out. Betty knew she didn't have much time to talk. Once in the helicopter she'd have access to a few more first aid tools and would be able to check Savannah out a little more thoroughly so she was ready for the hospital.

But she had to know… "Shay?"

"Bet… We'll talk in more detail when you're back at headquarters."

"Yeah, okay, but Garret?"

"He's fine. More than. He's out with Daniels. They're heading for HQ. Meet him there and you'll see for yourself."

"This is over?" Betty asked, not believing it was. Because Shay seemed…strange. Not herself. Though Betty couldn't put her finger on what seemed off.

There was the faintest hint of a pause before Shay said, "Yes."

Betty wanted to push Shay for more explanation. For the meaning behind that pause, but they had to get Savannah to the hospital.

Now.

# Chapter Fifteen

Garret wished the gnawing feeling something was terribly wrong would dissipate. But even as a man named Daniels led him into some kind of ranch house slash fortress, he felt nothing but a bundle of worry.

Allegedly, everything was fine. But he'd been through a North Star mission once before, and this didn't feel like *fine*. It most certainly didn't feel over. He'd been swept away from the aftermath, informed he'd be taken to North Star headquarters and reunited with his children.

He knew that was the important thing, so he'd gone along with it when Shay had ushered him into a Jeep with Daniels. Then they'd driven. And driven. And driven. Eventually, Garret had fallen asleep. Even when he'd woken up hours later, they were still driving.

Finally, they made it to an airport, where Daniels ushered him onto a tiny, old-looking plane. The pilot was a man Garret vaguely recognized from the aftermath of Nate's ordeal.

He flew them another few hours, and then landed on a grass field behind a large…luxury ranch house? Daniels led him off the plane, the pilot having said nothing.

Garret followed Daniels toward the house. After a few security measures, the back door opened and Garret was led into some kind of mudroom. Which then turned into a hallway, followed by a cozy-looking living room.

Where he finally recognized someone. Even if it was a bit of a shock to see Elsie, cross-legged on the couch, in her usual position hunched over a computer.

She looked up when Daniels cleared his throat. Then she jumped up and shocked Garret even more when she rushed over and threw her arms around him. "You're *safe.*"

Garret awkwardly patted her back. "Er. Yeah."

She pulled away, already talking a mile a minute. "I just couldn't stay in Blue Valley. Nate wanted to come, too, but I figured you'd want him taking care of your animals. Barney's so sad without you guys. Anyway, Nate wanted to get your dad involved, but I convinced him to just stay put. The fewer people involved, the better. And you'll be home soon." She smiled up at him. "Barney will be ecstatic."

"Thanks, Elsie. I'm glad." *Relieved.* He just didn't know how to explain any of this to his family. It was going to be hard enough with Mrs. Linley, his dispatcher at the police station.

"I've been helping with the babies. They're so sweet." She grabbed his hand and began pulling him across the room. "I know you're exhausted. We set you up in a room with them. You can look after them, or if you prefer one of our medics can look after them until you are ready to take over. Whatever you need, North Star is going to provide."

Garret didn't know what to say, so he simply let himself be led. Down a long hallway with lots of doors. Finally, she quietly pushed into one. The room was dark except for a dim lamp in the corner. A young woman sat in a rocking chair, looking at her phone.

She got up when Elsie entered. "Hey, Els. I assume this is Dad?"

"Yeah, Garret, this is Mara, one of our medics. She's been taking care of the kiddos since Gabriel dropped them off."

"They're in great shape. We played a little, ate. Now they're sleeping." She gestured to the crib in the corner.

Garret's chest tightened. His babies. Safe and sound. And Elsie had said they'd be able to go home soon. Back to his real life.

Except Betty wouldn't be there anymore. Her real life was here in this North Star headquarters.

"Maybe Mara should check out your shoulder," Elsie suggested.

Garret shook his head. He didn't know why the idea of someone besides Betty looking at his wound seemed…wrong. But it did. "I'm fine."

"You're exhausted, huh?" Elsie said, giving his arm a squeeze.

Garret blinked down at his arm. Exhausted. Maybe that's what was going through him. Maybe that explained how jumbled everything felt. "Uh, yeah, I guess so. Elsie, where's Betty?"

"She's on her way. It's a long way from Montana. I'm sure she'll look in on you guys when she gets here. You rest. Bed right there all made up for you. Phone on the nightstand, just press four and ask whoever answers for whatever you need. There's a bathroom right through there. You get hungry just call and someone can bring you something or take you to the kitchen. All three of you will be comfortable here, promise."

"Five-star service, huh?"

Elsie smiled. "We do what we can." She nodded to Mara, who walked over to the door. "Get some sleep, Garret. We can go over everything in the morning."

Garret nodded. He blew out a breath. This was all so strange, but he knew one thing for certain. "Elsie, thanks for being here. It means a lot to see a familiar face."

She reached up and gave him another friendly squeeze. "Anytime."

What exactly she saw in his brother, Garret would never know, but he was glad Nate had Elsie all the same.

She moved over to Mara and they exited the room together.

"He's not so bad to look at, is he?" the medic said in low tones that got lower as she and Elsie walked down the hall.

"I wouldn't look too hard. Betty's got her eyes on him."

They both laughed a little as their voices trailed off.

Betty had her eyes on him? Garret shook his head. He was probably hearing things. He closed the door behind them, then surveyed the dim room. A crib was in the corner, a big bed in the other. Everything he could want or need right here.

*Except Betty.*

He didn't know what he'd do when the babies woke up. They'd need changing, like Betty had shown him, but he hardly had it down. They'd need to be fed and

Garret didn't have the first clue how Betty had made the bottles or held them. Weren't you supposed to burp babies or something?

Elsie had said he could call for whatever he needed, but all he seemed to want was Betty at his side.

Which meant he *was* delirious. He wasn't sure he'd sleep the way his shoulder was throbbing, but he crawled into the bed anyway. He shouldn't be surprised it was comfortable. Everything about this place was a little too good to be true.

Just what *was* North Star? They'd helped his brother, but…was there more to it?

He closed his eyes and forced the thought out of his head. Everything was over. He and his children were safe. Betty would be here soon.

*And she'll stay right here while you go back to Montana.*

His eyes opened. He was surprised at the level of denial that swept through him. Betty had been a part of his life for a very brief…blip. He appreciated her. Barney was in some sort of doggie love with her, and these babies…

Garret purposefully closed his eyes again. He wasn't thinking straight, that was all. A few hours' sleep in a bed, some food when he woke up and some time holding his children… Things would start to make sense.

They had to.

"WE PUT HIM in the big room," Mara said, going through a list of things she was supposed to update Betty on. Betty hadn't heard the first few, but that one penetrated her current brain fog.

"He needs that gunshot wound looked at and likely rebandaged. You didn't check him out?"

"No. He said he was fine."

"Of course he did." Betty tried to keep the irritation out of her tone. Mara was a good medic, but she took things a little too personally still. Betty didn't want to get rid of her, not with her skills, but she wasn't sure she had the emotional wherewithal to stay on with North Star.

A problem for another day.

"Thanks, Mara. I'll handle it from here."

"Oh, but—"

Betty exited the room. Maybe she should have stayed and listened to Mara, but she was exhausted and she knew she wouldn't sleep until she'd checked in on Garret and the babies.

And heard back from Shay. Information on exactly what had happened wasn't…forthcoming, and something about all the silence and the unusual lack of a postmortem had dread settling in Betty's gut.

*One step at a time.*

She moved through North Star headquarters. It was a big building, outfitted with everything they needed. Elsie had a big computer room next to her quarters, and Betty had her office next to hers. Everyone else had their own bedrooms in the long hallway that also contained some open rooms for the rare times they needed to house someone in trouble.

There was a gym, a kitchen, meeting rooms and even an arcade room. Outside, there was the landing strip, and from anyone's POV it just looked like a wealthy person's second or third home, ensconced in the rolling Wyoming hills.

Betty had always liked it here—had liked getting out of South Dakota when their former headquarters had been burned down in an explosion. A new state had felt like a new start.

But then again, so had taking care of Garret in his sweet little house in Montana, with Barney. Which was beyond silly. She'd barely spent a few weeks there, and just because she missed that old mutt following her around meant nothing at all.

She stopped by her office and grabbed her cart of medical supplies, hoping the familiarity would settle her nerves. She often worked on operatives with minor injuries in their rooms to allow them privacy and comfort. No doubt Garret would appreciate it—he'd want to stay in the same room with his babies.

Safe. They were all *safe*. She wished she could let go of the anxiety still gripping her. Maybe once she checked Garret out she'd feel better.

She rolled the cart down the hall to the big room. The door was closed so she knocked quietly, just in case everyone was asleep. She gave it some time, then eased the door open.

The room was dark and she could hear the faint sound of snoring. But underneath that there was the soft, sweet sound of baby babble.

Betty left the cart in the hall and moved as quietly as possible over to where she knew the crib would be in the corner. She waited until her eyes adjusted to the dark. Based on sound and movement she could make out the shadow of one of the babies, wiggling just a little.

Betty reached out and stroked the baby's cheek. She could tell it was Maggie from the size. She placed her hand on her little belly. Maggie's hand patted Betty's gently, then little fingers wrapped around her pinky.

Everyone was safe. Betty wasn't sure why tears would spring to her eyes in this moment. The baby grasping her finger was a natural baby reaction. Relief and happiness were par for the course, but this was *bigger* than that, and she didn't have the words in her emotional vocabulary to explain it to herself. She could only feel bowled over by whatever it was.

"I'm glad you're safe and sound now," she whispered.

Betty heard a sharp intake of breath, the rustle of movement of a man waking up because someone was looming over his kids' crib.

"Just me," Betty said in a quiet, calm voice that would stop him from taking her out if he thought she was some kind of threat.

A light switched on and she looked over her shoulder at him. Garret was sitting on the edge of the bed. He was rubbing his eyes and yawning. He'd taken his shirt off at some point and she could clearly see he'd bled through his bandage.

She swallowed down the harsh words she wanted to hurl at him, if only because a little girl held her hand.

"You should have let someone check you out," Betty scolded. She scooped Maggie up and cradled her.

Garret looked down at the bandage. "Didn't notice."

"Liar. It hurt and you ignored it." She put Maggie down on the bed next to him. "She's such a quiet soul. You keep an eye on her there while I go get my supplies."

She didn't look at them together. Her heart was too

mushy right now to deal with the way Garret looked at his children. She got her cart and wheeled it in as quietly as possible.

Garret was attempting to pull a shirt over his head when she got close to the bed.

"Leave it off. I need to change that bandage. You'll be lucky if I don't have to redo the stitches."

He grunted and dropped the shirt. Betty focused on the bandage. Not on his big hand on Maggie's belly. Not on the way he gazed at the baby with a naked devotion that made her heart want to crack in two. No, she focused on pulling up the adhesive and examining the ways he'd done a number on the wound.

"Well, good news for you, it's healing pretty well. I think we can forgo redoing the stitches *if* you promise to take it easy." She wiped the shoulder down with antiseptic, then grabbed a new bandage.

"What does 'take it easy' entail?" he asked, grumpily. Reminding her of those first few days in his cabin. Here was not a man who would pretend everything was fine when it wasn't. But he'd still do what needed to be done—even sacrifice himself for the greater good. Not a martyr or a saint, just...

Oh, hell. It was ridiculous to be this gone over a guy she'd known a couple of weeks, but it seemed no amount of book smarts would allow her to talk herself out of how she felt. Still, no use *wallowing* in it. She had to focus on *Doctor* Betty. "Well, no hikes up mountains or at-gunpoint standoffs with bad guys. And no babies in this arm."

She smiled down at him, but his expression remained serious. His gaze steady on hers. "I guess I'll still need some help then for a while. Back home. Two babies, one arm."

Her breath caught in her throat, but she forced herself to push through it and speak even as her stomach swooped. It was stupid to want to be that help when she had a job to do here. Silly to think he might want *her* help when he had family and…community. "You will need some help yet," she agreed, and she had to study his wound. Intently. Rather than meet his gaze.

"Betty."

His voice was rough, and when she glanced at him again his eyes were full of…questions. Or maybe answers. Maybe she was the one with questions.

His free hand wrapped around her wrist where she was unnecessarily still smoothing down the bandage. She tried to maintain the eye contact, but she couldn't stay with that dark, certain gaze. Nothing inside of her felt very certain right now. She tried to find her doctor self in the midst of all this turmoil. Detached, casual calm.

But he repeated her name. Like she was supposed to understand what this was. Like she could control this tide of emotion inside of her. Like she knew at all what to do when he released her hand, touched her face and brought it down to his.

Like she could have any idea how to deal with his mouth touching hers, except to sink into it. Because surely this was a dream or hallucination born of exhaustion and all that they'd been through the past day or two.

He couldn't actually be kissing her. It couldn't actually be ten times better than anything she had imagined. And yes, she *had* spent some serious time imagining.

There was so much inside of her and she didn't know what to do with it all. But more than that, mostly there was just him. Too good, down to the core. And a kiss that obliterated anything else. Too big. Too much. Too fast. She didn't go down those roads where it was too easy to get lost. She stood on her own two feet. Always.

Always.

She pulled away. From his mouth, from his hand on hers. She took a full step back and looked at the floor rather than him. "I'm sure that was some sort of… delirium."

"No, just something I've been wanting to do for a while."

Her eyes flew up to meet his. She wasn't *surprised* exactly. There'd been a little hum of…electricity or attraction or whatever it was from the very beginning. *A while*. But there was something alarming at how… serious and *deep* it felt. Voicing it for the first time instead of…uncertain looks.

Especially here in this room with his kids, knowing he'd trusted her to save them. But that's all this was, wasn't it? Some kind of warped…savior thing.

It stung, like a wound she wasn't sure she'd known she had. "I don't need that kind of gratitude."

"Gratitude?" He snorted. "I hardly think me having feelings for you is *gratitude*. If I had *gratitude*, I'd stay the hell away. I should stay the hell away."

"Why?"

He swept his hand to encompass the room. "This isn't how you…" He trailed off, shaking his head. "My life is a mess. You don't start something in the wreckage you have to rebuild."

"Seems to me that's exactly when you start something," she couldn't seem to stop herself from saying.

His mouth curved, ever so slightly. "So, Bet, you want to start something?"

She swallowed. Fear threatened to consume her, because weren't good things always ten times scarier than the bad? So much harder to hold on to. To make right.

"You can say no."

"I don't want to say no," she managed through her too-tight throat. *No* to him and his kids and his dog? No, she didn't want to say no to any of that. She just didn't know how to say yes. To a man like him. To a life like his. Starting didn't mean ending. She knew that all too well.

But she couldn't imagine walking away. Wasn't this what she and Shay had stood next to each other and talked about back at that airport? Building something for once.

"Admit it, you're just after my dog."

It took her a moment, for the reality of the situation to sink in. He'd made a joke. A real joke. This stoic, at times grumpy, far-too-good man.

"You're onto me," she croaked. "The kids help your case, too."

He inhaled, and she noticed that his hand had never left Maggie, lying there quietly on the blanket. "It's a lot. You've got North Star."

"I do." She frowned. North Star had felt like it was falling apart lately—Shay's words, though Betty would call it something else. Moving on, maybe. But the reminder of Shay and everything that didn't sit right with the way this had ended was a new problem. "Garret, something isn't right here. I know we're safe. I should feel more settled or something. But Shay…"

Garret's expression sobered and seeing her own concern mirrored on his face had her stomach sinking. "She was acting weird," he confirmed.

"Yes. *Yes.*" If Garret saw it, too, it had to be something.

He nodded. "So we'll figure it out. Before we head back to Blue Valley. We'll figure it out."

Betty studied him. *We.* Yeah, she couldn't say no to a chance at that. "And then we'll figure us out."

"Us," Garret repeated. Then Cain started crying, no quiet gurgles for him. He went into a full wail the moment he woke up.

Betty moved to pick him up. "This one is going to give you some trouble," Betty said fondly, cuddling him to her chest. "Maggie might play calm and serene, but those are the girls you have to watch out for." She turned to face Garret.

He was staring at her. So serious again. "I like you an awful lot."

Her heart fluttered. "Well, the feeling is mutual."

He smiled. One of those rare full-blown ones. "Good. Now maybe you can teach me how to make a bottle so we can feed these two."

She nodded, not trusting her voice. Not trusting anything. Except that he'd said they'd figure it out.

*One step at a time.*

## Chapter Sixteen

Garret had no idea what he was doing. He figured that was a good first step, because once upon a time he'd known exactly what he was doing. Down to the letter. Everything had blown up in his face then.

So this time around, he'd go with his gut.

His gut told him Betty was someone to hold on to. Especially when the good doctor got that deer-in-the-headlights look about her. Not always quite so in control of things.

Yeah, his gut liked that quite a bit.

They changed the kids' diapers and then she led him to a kitchen area and talked him through making the bottles, all while she held Cain and he held Maggie. Partners.

His shoulder still hurt, but he didn't mind it. Especially since he still needed a doctor's care—*this* doctor's care.

Maybe Betty would end up heading back to North Star. Maybe whatever they started would end quickly enough. He was under no illusions he could predict the future, or that feelings were constant. He had one spectacularly failed marriage under his belt after all.

But he also had these two miracles. Cain and Maggie. His.

So a chance was enough.

Betty took him to a living room area and pointed him to an armchair. She talked about the best angle to hold the bottle, talked him through burping and something called tummy time. He felt faintly ridiculous, but she was so matter-of-fact about reading to them even though they couldn't have a damn clue what he was saying.

"How do you know so much about what to do? You're a doctor for adults, aren't you?"

"I'm technically in family practice. I did some work in emergency medicine, too, and then being with North Star I've sort of…honed a lot of different skills that a respectable medical establishment wouldn't probably recognize as legitimate."

"And you keep avoiding the main question."

Betty played with the edges of the blanket the babies were spread out on. He'd rarely seen her flustered or uncomfortable, but it was these personal things that made her squirmy. Feelings. Her past.

"Tell me, Bet."

She tried to smile, but it didn't reach her eyes. And she didn't look at him.

"My father was a doctor for a…" She trailed off, eyebrows drawing together. "Well, a gang, to be honest."

She slid him a glance, clearly looking for some kind of reaction. Maybe it was because he was a cop or just because of what she'd dealt with in her life that she expected him to have one, but he'd dealt with a lot of people's sad childhood stories. He kept his expression neutral. "You grew up in a gang?" he asked, carefully calm and even—like she was when she was in doctor mode.

"Not *in* it, exactly. More on the fringes. Dad tried to protect me as much as he could. Keep us separate. But a lot of the kids there didn't get treated very well, especially when they were this age." Betty pointed to the babies. "They were helpless. So to the gang they were useless. Dad and I did our best to…take care of who we could."

"Where was your mother?"

Betty's expression shuttered. Her gaze stayed on the babies. "She wasn't really in the picture." Betty chewed on her bottom lip for a moment, then she got to her feet. "I'm going to call the hospital again. See if there are any updates on Savannah."

Garret nodded. Betty stepped out of the room and he played with the babies, lying on the floor with them and reading to them or tickling them. Marveling, over and over again, that they were his.

When Betty returned, Garret couldn't read her expression.

"She's in a coma," Betty said matter-of-factly. "Alive, but… The chances aren't great. Possible, but not great."

Garret kept thinking at some point he'd know what to feel. About Savannah. Being alive. Purposefully luring him into danger. Using his babies against him. And yet…he hadn't been able to leave her to die.

Garret looked down at Maggie, who was on her back, trying to grab her toes. Cain was on his stomach, lifting his little head and trying to get a lay of the land. They made quiet noises, seemingly talking in their own language to each other.

Savannah was their mother. He couldn't...change that any more than he could change what she'd done.

"She saved me," Betty said, earnestly. "That guy would have come back and... Well, I don't really want to think about what he had planned. I know you're conflicted, but you and your kids deserve to know she did something right. Even before I helped her—"

"You saved her. Just as she saved you."

"Okay, maybe I did," Betty acquiesced. "But she saved me first."

"You didn't know that when you went about trying to help her," Garret returned. It wasn't that he wanted to think Savannah was a monster. He'd much rather think there was a decent part of her. It just...wasn't the same.

Betty took a deep breath. "Okay. Put all that aside. You asked about my mother? She was in that gang. She was not a good person. So I know what it's like. To grow up with the mother who wasn't around. Who I *knew* was out there doing bad things. My mother never did *anything* good. It...hurts. Knowing that. Growing up with that. Savannah did something right. Give your kids the gift of knowing, even if she ended up being in the wrong a lot of the time, she did something right sometimes."

It was a lot to take in, but clearly it meant a lot to her. So he really...thought about it. Didn't just give her a trite answer. "I guess I have time to work it all out. But I hear what you're saying."

She smiled sadly, giving him a vague nod. He held out his hand and she stared at it a moment before she took it. He pulled her over to him and she knelt down next to him. He didn't have the words, but if he followed that gut feeling again, he didn't think that's what she needed.

He slid his arm around her shoulders. Squeezed. They sat like that, watching the babies for a few content, quiet moments. After a while, the words seemed to find themselves.

"I had a pretty good childhood, but I've seen a lot of the bad people can do in my job. I understand. Maybe not as deeply as some people might, but I understand what seeing the bad can do. The way it wears on you when you can't stop it. How you just have to keep doing the next…right thing to combat that feeling. If nothing else, I want them to know that."

She brushed her lips across his cheek. "That's a pretty good 'if nothing else.'" She leaned her head on his shoulder, letting out a breath that relaxed her posture.

They sat like that, relaxed and wrapped in each other, watching the kids. If he could look forward to this…

But that thought was interrupted when Elsie bustled into the room. Betty stiffened a little and lifted her head off his shoulder.

If there was any surprise, Elsie didn't show it.

"Is Shay back yet?" Betty asked.

"No," Elsie said, worrying her bottom lip. "She didn't answer when I called, either."

Betty shook her head, concern taking over her expression. Garret might not know Shay that well, but he was worried, too. None of this settled right.

"How long do we wait?" Garret asked.

Betty and Elsie exchanged a look of women who'd worked together a long time and knew each other quite well.

"As long as it takes," they said in unison.

BETTY KNEW GARRET wasn't satisfied with her and Elsie's nonanswer. She wasn't satisfied, either. But what neither she nor Elsie were willing to say out loud—in front of Garret or even to each other—was that Shay was the leader. She was in charge. Without her...

No one knew quite who to turn to. It would be different if Reece was still here, or Holden. Or if Sabrina was up for more than her daily walks around the compound.

"We could call Granger," Elsie said in a whisper as they stood in the kitchen putting together some dinner for everyone.

"Shay definitely wouldn't want us to do that."

"She isn't *here*. And she told Daniels it might be a while, but this is longer than a while. We can't just sit here twiddling our thumbs." Elsie scowled. "This isn't like her. We have to do something."

Betty agreed, but her loyalty to Shay overrode everything she knew and felt. "You're only saying that because you want to get home to your boyfriend."

Elsie shot her an *oh, really* look. "And don't you want to head on to Blue Valley with me so you can cuddle up with my boyfriend's brother?"

Betty managed to chuckle even though the Shay situation made it hard to really feel good or happy, even about Garret. "Maybe."

"Pfft." Elsie nudged Betty with her elbow. "What I walked into was downright *sweet*."

It had been. Sweet and nice and… He'd said what she'd needed to hear. An understanding she hadn't expected to find in a man who seemed so…good. A man willing to lay down his life…

Yeah, she wasn't ready to think about that right now. Too much was up in the air. Way too much.

She heard the commotion in the hallway before she could think of anything else to say. Both her and Elsie forgot the salad they were making and moved to see what it was.

Shay was walking, surrounded by Connor, Mallory and even Sabrina. They were crowded around Shay, but Shay kept walking. Elsie and Betty joined in, trailing after them all.

Betty noted Sabrina, who'd almost *died* not all that long ago, was walking around without the walker she was supposed to use.

"Sabrina Killian. Where the hell is your walker?" Betty demanded, even as relief over Shay being back swamped her.

Sabrina angled her body to show that Connor had his arm firmly around her. "This oaf is my walker."

Betty wanted to scold both of them more, but everyone else was shooting questions at Shay as she kept walking down the hallway, and even Betty had to forget about Sabrina not following medical orders.

Eventually, Shay seemed to have had enough of the questions and people following her. She stopped abruptly and held up her hands. Everyone stopped demanding answers and waited expectantly.

Shay looked at all of them. Betty couldn't read the expression or even begin to predict what Shay would say.

"We'll meet in the conference room in fifteen," she said after a moment. She craned her head to look through the faces crowded around her. "Bet?"

"Yeah?"

"Bring Garret. Have one of the medics look after the babies." She dropped her hand. "I'm going to run through the shower. Unless you want a show, I suggest you all stay here."

She walked down the hall toward her room, and everyone stood where they were. Sharing looks.

But no one said anything. No one knew what to say. Eventually, they all started heading toward the conference room. Betty got Mara to stay with the babies and grabbed Garret and brought him to the conference room.

Almost exactly fifteen minutes later Shay strode into the conference room. She went to the front of the room and stood there, facing the small group of people. Per usual, Elsie was at her computer. Chairs were filled with all the lead field operatives, along with Mallory and Gabriel, and a few of the other agents who'd been on this mission.

Garret sat at the end of one of the rows of people, and Betty stood by the door like she usually did. Because she was rarely involved in these meetings. Usually she slipped out, but this one...

She couldn't.

Shay didn't need to wait for anyone to be quiet. Everyone was already silent, waiting for answers. Waiting for the last forty-eight hours to make some sense.

"To recap," Shay began, all eyes on her, "Cliff Jenkins is in police custody now that the hospital has released him. Savannah Loren is still in the hospital. Should she recover, we'll start talking with the police about what we've got." Her eyes landed on Garret for a moment. "Or don't got, depending."

*Cliff Jenkins.* That must have been the man who'd shot Savannah. And if he'd already been released from the hospital, that meant he had recovered quickly.

Shay said nothing else. Again, looks were exchanged. Gabriel nudged Connor and Sabrina gave him a little nod. Eventually, Connor stood. "Before she passed out, Savannah said a name. Obviously, I don't know that it means anything, but if we're still looking for some answers, maybe the name is a clue."

Shay went very still. She eyed Connor with a distance Betty didn't recognize. Not leader to subordinate. Not even old hat to rookie field operative. A stillness and watchfulness Betty couldn't work out.

"And the name was?" Shay asked casually.

"Vianni."

Shay didn't move. Betty wasn't even sure she breathed. Betty had known Shay for almost a decade now. They were both one of the few people of North Star who'd been around since almost the beginning.

But Betty had no idea what her friend was thinking or feeling.

It was terrifying.

"Well, we can do a cursory search on that name if Elsie wants." Shay looked down at the table in front of her as if she was studying information. But there was only a blank table. "All the main players are in custody, one way or another, so I'm not sure we need to worry about it."

"It wasn't just Savannah and this Cliff guy," Garret said, clearly not worried about protocol or seniority the way some of the operatives in the room were.

"Ringleaders," Shay replied. "We rounded up a few of their team. Mostly for-hire muscle. Not much to follow up on. Vianni is an old mafia family we took down years ago. They've been eradicated for a long time."

Betty watched Garret this time. His expression was a little easier to read. He didn't buy what Shay was saying. Betty surveyed the rest of the faces she knew so well.

Not one person on the North Star team looked altogether convinced of what Shay was saying. Something Betty couldn't ever remember happening—even when Shay first started as leader. Not everyone had been *excited* about the change in leadership, but they'd trusted her. Believed in her.

What had happened out there in the Montana wilderness?

"For now, we wait on the hospital reports on Savannah," Shay said. "So we'll sit close and tight. You're all dismissed."

It took a moment. A long, tense moment for anyone to move. Sabrina did first, and since Connor had to help her, he got to his feet. Slowly, everyone trailed out of the conference room. Except Betty, Elsie and Garret.

"Was there something you three needed?"

Elsie hesitated. "No. I just thought…" Elsie looked at Garret then back at Shay. "You said sit close. Can't Garret and I go back to Blue Valley?"

Garret stood himself.

"I know I'd like to get back to Blue Valley and get the twins settled. And if you can spare her, I'd like Betty to

come with. Truth be told, I can't take care of two kids
with my shoulder banged up like this."

"Don't you have parents to help you?"

Betty was more than a little surprised. She hadn't
expected pushback, not when Shay had been overly accommodating about the gunshot wound Garret had re-
ceived helping *them*. Not when she'd practically been
pushing Elsie out the door to stay in Blue Valley and
start a real life for herself.

"Shay, he needs a medical professional," Betty said,
wondering if Shay was in a misplaced way trying to
protect Betty. "At least for a while longer. You've got
Mara and the rest of my team here if you're running
any more missions. Unless there's something you're not
telling me, you can spare me."

Shay's gaze flicked to Betty. There was a…coldness
there, almost. Something odd and off and clearly proving that, no matter what Betty had hoped, this *wrong*
feeling wasn't going away just because Shay was back.

"Like I said. Everyone stays close and tight for the
time being. I'll let you know when you're free to go."

Then she strode out of the room before anyone could
question her further. Garret, Betty and Elsie exchanged
looks.

But Elsie was the one to say what they were all thinking. "Something is very, very wrong."

"It has to do with that Vianni name. Don't you
think?" Garret said, posing the question to Betty.

Much as she hated to admit it, that's exactly what
she thought. "Yeah. Els?"

Elsie sat down at her computer once more. "Shay's

right. We got rid of them years ago. They had a connection to the Sons and the explosion."

Betty nodded. She remembered the name, and the
Viannis being taken down. Just like the Sons.

"I'll look into it all the same. Maybe it's some new
faction or something."

Betty nodded. Maybe. Whatever it was, Betty had
the sinking suspicion Shay was going to do whatever
it took to keep it a secret.

# Chapter Seventeen

Garret had been living with this low-level feeling of things being wrong for a while now. Not just the past few days, but all those months since Savannah had disappeared. No matter how he'd tried to wrestle his life back into control, he hadn't been able to manage.

And now he was stuck in some secret group's headquarters, with his twin babies, and a woman he was...

She'd said it was the best time to build something, and he couldn't get that out of his head. He'd always waited for the perfect timing before. Always built the foundation first.

And didn't those foundations always crumble?

He shook his head. There were bigger things to think about. Like home and the fact he couldn't go there. He picked up the phone next to the bed while Maggie and Cain were sleepily distracted by the tinkling mobile above the crib. He dialed Nate's number.

"Hey, Garret," Nate answered. "Elsie already told me you guys are stuck there for a while."

"Yeah. Stuck all right." And that just didn't sit well, no matter how many different ways he tried to swallow it. "How are the animals?"

"Good enough. Horses are good, though Dad's been sniffing around some wondering why he hasn't seen you. Mom and Dad aren't buying the vacation thing any more than Mrs. Linley is. But they don't have a clue what it is you're really doing or that you were shot, so I guess you're in the clear as much as you can be."

Garret looked at his babies. "For now."

"Barney's been sleeping on the guest bed and refusing to leave except to eat. I tried to take him into the station today, but he wasn't having any of it."

The guest bed. In other words, Betty's bed. If that wasn't a sign she belonged, what was? Garret studied the room around him. Nice, sure. But not his. "I'm not part of this group. I don't have to follow their rules."

"No, but listen… I know Elsie can take care of herself, and has, but if the two of you could just kind of stick together until someone figures out what's up with Shay, I'd appreciate it."

The bedroom door creaked open and Betty stepped inside with that damn medical cart. He frowned at it.

"Garret?"

"Yeah, I'll do my best. Thanks for looking after everything. Appreciate it."

"No problem. See you soon."

"Yeah. Bye." Soon. He wanted it to be soon. He was completely over being involved in North Star business that had nothing to do with him. He turned to Betty. "Did Elsie find anything about this Vianni name?"

Betty shook her head. "Nothing new. She's combing through a lot of old information to see if something pops up."

"I don't want to stay here, but—"

She crossed to him, resting her hands on his fore-arms. "I know North Star isn't your problem, Garret. You absolutely deserve to go home. But this is my family. My life. If you could just—"

*"But,"* he continued, touching her face because if nothing else was right, being in the same room with her and being able to touch her was. "Nate asked me to keep an eye on Elsie, even if she didn't need it. So I figure I better stick around."

Her shoulders relaxed. "I just think if Shay wants to keep us close there's a reason, and likely it has to do with our own safety."

"This doesn't connect to Nate anymore. Does it?"

Betty looked up at him, her expression full of worry and confusion. "Elsie and I talked about that. If it did, she'd want him here. If it did... I know Savannah connected to Nate's military stuff, but I think..."

"She's gotten into something else. Something over her head."

Betty nodded. "The man in that house wanted North Star. Now, maybe that's because of what went down with Nate. But neither you nor I nor Nate was his target. He wants to *hurt* North Star. Not just kill people. Cause pain and suffering. He wants some kind of revenge. That's what he said to me."

"And you told all that to Shay?"

Betty shook her head. "I *tried*. She didn't want to listen." Betty began to pace. "This is what I don't get. She's shut down. Shut this case off. Wants none of the information she'd normally be poring over."

"She must know more than she's letting on."

Betty plopped onto the edge of the bed, looking lost

and a little desperate. He crossed over to her, but Cain began to cry.

"Rest that shoulder," Betty ordered, getting back to her feet. She walked over to the crib and picked up Cain. She gave Maggie's cheek a gentle stroke. "They're good sleepers," Betty said, swaying Cain back and forth. "He fights it, but once he's out, he's out."

Garret's heart squeezed painfully, a glimpse into something he hadn't planned on. Not her or them. But it all seemed too perfect. Except they were *here*, not home.

"We can't sit around and wait. We have to figure this out. I know Shay's your boss—"

"And my friend," Betty interrupted. "I love her like a sister. I'd do anything for her."

Before Garret could try to argue with her, she shushed him. Gently, she placed Cain back in the crib and then stepped over to Garret. She took him by the arm and led him to the bed, nudging him until he sat. She pulled the cart over and he scowled at her. "Didn't you just change this?"

"Hours ago," she said in a low whisper. "Until it stops bleeding, it needs to be changed three times a day. So stop complaining and listen to me."

He grunted in return while she got everything together. Since he was wearing a T-shirt, she just pushed the sleeve up and began to take off one bandage and replace it.

"I would do anything for Shay," she repeated after a while. "But that's the problem. I think Shay's in trouble. I want to help her."

A rap sounded on the door and Betty smoothed the bandage on his shoulder before going to answer it.

Elsie stepped inside and Betty held her finger to her lips. Elsie looked over at the crib and nodded. Then the three of them huddled together, talking as quietly as they could.

"Vianni?" Garret asked.

Elsie shook her head. "Nothing new on Vianni yet, but…" Elsie trailed off and looked around the room. "One sec." She moved to the phone and turned it over, flipping some kind of switch on it. She studied a panel on the wall Garret had thought was some kind of outdated communication system, but Elsie fooled with some switches and then turned to Garret sheepishly. "It's not like we *have* been listening to you. It's just all the rooms have that capability. I want to make sure no one hears me say this."

"What is it?" Betty asked, all concerned.

"Shay is telling different people different stories."

"What do you mean?"

"She told Gabriel the for-hire guys were old Sons cronies. She told Mallory they worked for that Cliff Jenkins specifically. She told Daniels Savannah wasn't going to make it and Mara that she was awake—when we all know she's in a coma."

"Why would she do that?" Betty asked.

"I don't understand it. She's not confused. She has to be doing it for a reason."

Garret's heart sank. *He* knew the reason. He hated to tell these women, who clearly didn't want to think it of their secret group, but there was no time to spare their feelings. "She thinks there's a leak."

Both women gave him twin looks of confusion.

"You spread false information to either cause confusion, and I don't know why she'd do that," Garret explained. "Or to see what information gets out to the people you don't want it to get out to."

"There's no leak in North Star," Elsie said firmly. "I would know."

Garret considered how much he wanted to have this argument. An argument he knew Elsie had had with Nate back when they were dealing with his thing. But this didn't have to do with Nate. Or the military. This was about Shay and North Star specifically.

"That man knew who and what North Star was, and Shay was rattled enough to think if we didn't take him down, everyone at North Star was at risk. Not just everyone with North Star now, anyone who had ever worked for North Star."

"Wait. What?"

"That's what she told me when she sent me in there. She couldn't risk her people, or it had the potential to end the lives of too many."

Elsie blew out a long, slow breath. "I've got to keep poring over those old records."

"But we got him," Betty pointed out. "And clearly she's not worried…" Betty trailed off as it dawned on her.

"She is worried. That's why we're not going home," Garret said grimly.

Betty looked back at the crib, eyebrows drawn together. "About that… I have an idea."

IT HAD BEEN forming ever since Shay had been acting so strangely in that conference room. Even before Betty had understood…or been ready to face what was before her, she'd known Shay was in trouble and it would be up to those who knew her best to help.

Shay would want to handle it on her own, and maybe she could. But Betty had a bad feeling that the way things were going meant she couldn't.

Garret's theories only added to how much Betty felt they needed to do this. Get to the bottom of things. Help Shay.

She could turn it over to an operative, but that would be too easy for Shay to pick up on. Shay wouldn't expect it from her and Elsie. She wouldn't be able to predict what a doctor and tech guru were going to do.

"It's risky, and rather out of character for me," Betty continued. She knew she had Garret and Elsie's rapt attention, but it was hard to go against…everything. Her usual role at North Star, her area of expertise, and her love for and loyalty to Shay.

But this was *for* Shay. If there *was* a leak… "We would have found a leak. With Nate's stuff. We would have figured that out."

"There was no leak," Elsie said firmly. "I know that."

"So what about an old leak? If this man was threatening North Star past and present, maybe it isn't about the now."

"An old leak?" Elsie repeated, clearly thinking it over.

"This is about North Star, except Shay is keeping it to herself. What does that tell you?"

Elsie nodded, as if starting to understand Betty's thought process. "It's about her more than the group."

"Exactly." She turned to Garret, needing him to see

the depth of understanding she was working from, so he would trust her instincts. What they needed to do.

"Shay and I started at North Star pretty much together. I've patched her up almost more than anyone else. I know her. She's probably my best friend in the world, but when you're North Star, your past disappears. I've mentioned pieces of my past to Shay, but voluntarily. She's never done the same. I don't know where she came from."

"Okay," Garret said when Betty paused, clearly waiting for more.

"We, as a group, worked to take down the gang my dad worked for and my mom was a part of. The Sons of the Badlands. A lot of us had ties to them. A lot of us wanted a kind of revenge, I guess, or a righting of wrongs. I always assumed Shay did, too."

"I didn't have a connection, though," Elsie said, frowning. She looked at Betty. "It wasn't a requirement. Granger wanted the best minds when he built North Star."

"Yes, for tech and medical stuff. For administration."

"Shay's been everything—well, not a doctor, but she's worked in all the other arms."

Betty nodded. "That's what I'm trying to say. I don't know what her past was like, but this could connect to a time before she joined. If there's a leak or a connection, it's personal to her. It's not about the group. It's about *her*."

Elsie bobbed her head up and down as Betty spoke. "That makes a lot of sense."

"There are two people I can think of who might have answers to some of these questions."

"Granger," Elsie said.

Betty nodded. "But…I can't explain why I think that's the wrong route to go down right now. There's too much… Granger is still too wrapped up in North Star no matter how hard he pretends not to be. There's… I don't want to call it bad blood between them…"

"Tension, then."

"Yeah. We need to work this carefully. Maybe eventually we go to Granger, but for now we need a more… separate hand."

Elsie's forehead wrinkled. "Then who?"

"Cody."

"Cody Wyatt?" Elsie's eyes widened. "You think he'd talk to us behind Shay's back?"

"If we can convince him Shay is in trouble? He'll talk, or his wife will." She turned to Garret. "Cody was an old operative. He worked with Shay a lot before he quit, and Shay's close with him and his wife still."

"So…how?"

Betty inhaled. "That's the part of the plan I don't really know about. We can't call. We have to go."

"Shay told us to sit tight."

"I know." Betty looked from Elsie to Garret. The three of them could do it. With Elsie's tech expertise, and Garret's cop background. Elsie knew Cody, but not as well as Betty did. The three of them could get to Cody and see if he had any information.

She didn't know how to verbalize the plan, but it seemed she didn't have to. "If there's a leak, a threat to North Star, we can't leave them here," Garret said, pointing to the sleeping twins.

"No, we can't. But I know somewhere we could where they'd be safe."

Garret looked at his sleeping babies, then at Betty. He blew out a breath. "I'll have to trust you on that, Bet."

"We'll have to trust each other. This is going rogue. Shay will be ticked off. It could be dangerous. We don't know what we're getting into. It's a risk, and if anyone's unsure—"

"I'm sure," Elsie said. "We need to do this."

Betty looked at Garret, and he nodded grimly. "Agreed."

Betty swallowed down the nerves and the fear, because apparently she was now in charge of a secret mission. "Elsie, you'll have to find a way for us to get out of here without anyone knowing. Garret, pack up everything we'll need for the kids. I'll pack my medical bag. Can we get out of here within the hour?"

"We'll do our best," Elsie said.

All Betty could do was hope their best was good enough.

## Chapter Eighteen

It took some time to get everything situated. Mostly they had to wait on Elsie to tamper with some security and arrange for transportation that North Star wouldn't easily be able to track.

Then they had to wait for the middle of the night, when they were confident everyone was asleep. So they could slip out undetected. Of course, people would know once everyone started waking up, but if they could get a couple hours' head start, Elsie and Betty were pretty confident it would take people a while to figure out their plan.

Garret took the first shift driving, while Elsie tapped away at her computer in the passenger seat and Betty played with the babies in the back, since they hadn't fallen asleep after being transferred to the car.

They arrived in a small Wyoming town at the break of day, and Garret followed Betty's directions out of town, onto a highway turnoff, and then to the front of a…

"It's a bed-and-breakfast?"

"Yes," Betty said.

Elsie looked up from her computer.

"Anything?" Garret asked.

She rubbed her eyes and shook her head. "No. Every major player in the Vianni family is in jail or dead."

Cain began to wail, quickly followed by a rare display of temper from Maggie. All the adults in the car moved into action, getting the babies out of the car. Garret held Cain in his good arm and Elsie bounced Maggie on her hip while Betty collected everything she'd packed for them.

Garret hung back while Elsie and Betty started moving toward the house. It looked like a postcard, down to the sign decorated with bluebirds that said Bluebird Inn. And it certainly was isolated.

Still, he didn't like the idea of leaving his children with strangers after these merry-go-round days. He wanted to get them home.

But they all had to be safe first.

"Reece used to work with North Star. He was Shay's right-hand man. Lead agent. So he'll know what to watch for and how to keep the kids safe," Betty said in low tones as Elsie knocked on the door. "His wife already has one kid and is pregnant with the second, so she knows the ins and outs of taking care of babies. And this place is isolated and protected. It's the best place for them."

Garret nodded. He wasn't sure it eased his nerves any, but he trusted Betty to do the best thing for the twins. Always.

A blonde woman answered the door with a warm smile. "Good morning, guys. Come on in."

Elsie stepped in first and the woman held out her arms for Maggie. Maggie went without hesitation and something in Garret's chest loosened. They all stepped into a kitchen area, where a tall, broad man stood military straight and a young boy in superhero pajamas peeked his blond head around him.

"Look at you," Betty said, the affection in her voice warm as she reached out and touched the woman's slightly rounded stomach. "Glowing."

"Thanks, Betty." She cuddled Maggie to her chest.

"Garret, this is Lianna, Reece and Henry Montgomery," Betty said, pointing to the woman, the man and then the boy. "This is Garret Averly. The twins' father."

"They'll be safe here," Reece said. And something about the way he stood and said those words with a grave authority helped Garret relax his shoulders.

Garret looked at his babies. Twin dark eyes staring at him. He'd had them for such a short time, it seemed wrong to leave them. But he wanted them home. Where they belonged, which meant he had to make that a safe option.

"Can I hold one?" Henry asked, gazing up at Cain with open curiosity. He made a silly face at the baby and Cain reached out and tried to tug his hair.

"In a minute, Henry," Lianna said to her son. "They'll be safe *and* loved on," Lianna assured him with a warm smile.

Garret cleared his throat. "Thanks."

"We need to move quickly," Betty said, her hand coming to rest on his back. A reassurance that this wasn't a forever kind of goodbye.

But it was hard. He looked down at Cain in his arms and...

He was doing this for them. So they'd be safe. And

he was doing this for the woman who'd saved them. Gotten them to freedom back in that cabin. Someday, they'd understand that.

Garret kissed Cain's forehead, whispered reassurances to the boy, then handed him off to Reece. He repeated the goodbye process with Maggie.

It would have been impossible to walk out of that house, leaving his babies behind, but Betty slipped her hand in his. That small, warm reminder of who and what he was doing this for.

"Check in whenever you'd like," Lianna said kindly as they trailed reluctantly back outside.

Garret inhaled the cool, country morning air and didn't look back, though he desperately wanted to. He held on to Betty's hand like an anchor and walked back for their car. "Now where?" he asked, his voice rougher than he wanted it to be.

But Betty didn't comment. "We have to get to Cody. I don't think Shay will expect it, but we'll have to drive. It's going to take some time, but it's the best option I can think of."

Elsie nodded, walking next to Betty.

"Okay. I'll take the first shift since I won't be able to sleep. Where am I driving to?" Garret slid into the car as Betty got into the passenger seat and Elsie into the back.

"Bonesteel, South Dakota. It's about a six- or seven-hour drive, depending on traffic. Headquarters will know we're gone before we get there, but I don't think they'll anticipate where we're going."

Garret nodded, reminding himself why they were doing this. He understood Elsie and Betty needed to do this for their friend and because it was…well, their family. Clearly Betty didn't have a relationship with her mother if she was still alive, and he presumed her father was dead. Elsie had her sisters, but she, too, had gotten pretty worthless parents. Their community was North Star and their sister, so to speak, was in trouble.

So they started the drive to South Dakota.

BETTY BLINKED HER eyes open and yawned, trying to stretch out her cramped neck. She'd fallen asleep in the back seat. Elsie had taken over driving about halfway when Garret's eyelids had started to droop. They'd had to fight him on it, but he was now snoozing in the front seat.

A much-needed snooze. Betty would need to change his bandage again. She looked next to her, expecting to see the car seats before she remembered they'd dropped the babies off. It left an ache in her heart. For Garret, and knowing how hard it had been to say goodbye to them again. But also for herself. There was something… life-altering about taking care of those two.

But she didn't have time to think too much on that. They were driving into Bonesteel on a sunny afternoon.

It was an unassuming town. Maybe even smaller than Blue Valley. There weren't very many houses, and a very small, abbreviated Main Street. Elsie drove down to the end of it, right where it reconnected with the highway, to the two-story stone building that had a sign on the front that read one simple word.

*Computers.*

Cody didn't just deal in computers, but there weren't

very many people who knew that. Elsie drove around back and parked next to a big truck.

Elsie looked back at Betty when she parked. A clear sign Elsie was leaving waking Garret up to her. Betty nudged his good shoulder carefully and Garret immediately became alert. He took in the building before them.

"This it?" he asked, his voice rusty with sleep.

"This is it."

They all got out of the car and Betty took the lead, going to the back door that was the house entrance. She knocked and waited.

Nina, heavily pregnant, answered, her blond hair pulled back in a ponytail, her hand resting on her belly. She blinked once, the only sign she was surprised or taken off guard. "Well, hi, guys. Long time no see. Come on in."

They were ushered into the kitchen. "Let me go find Cody," Nina said, looking at Elsie, then Betty, then Garret hanging back by the door. She smiled, but it was thin.

Betty couldn't blame her. Cody had left North Star and danger behind. Who wanted it crashing into their kitchen on a pretty Saturday afternoon?

But before Nina could exit the kitchen, Cody's voice echoed from somewhere deeper in the house.

"Nina, I can't find the…" He trailed off as he came to the kitchen and saw the three of them. Like his wife, Cody blinked once. His expression remained very carefully passive. "Betty. Elsie. What brings you by?"

"Don't worry. Nothing terrible has happened and we don't need your help, at least not in the way you're probably thinking. No one's followed us. Or even knows we're here. We just need some information," Betty said, hoping the rush of assurances would set them at *some* ease.

"Is it Shay?" Nina asked, worry wrinkling her brow.

"Why do you ask that?" Garret asked.

"And who are you?" Cody returned, not hiding the edge to his voice.

"This is Garret. He's helping us. And yes, Nina. This has to do with Shay. We need—"

"Daddy!" Cody's oldest daughter skidded to a stop in the kitchen. She looked around at all the adults in the room. She smiled at Elsie and Betty, but there was also a knowing glance at her parents. The ten-year-old knew how to recognize danger.

"Can you go play with your sister for a bit, Brianna?" Cody said, resting his hand on top of the girl's head. "Mom and I will be finished in just a few minutes, okay? Don't worry."

Brianna nodded. She gave Betty and Elsie a wave and then headed back into the deeper part of the house.

Cody's placid expression immediately changed to frustration as his focus went from his daughter to the trio of intruders in his house. "I don't understand why you're here. A doctor and a tech specialist. Why isn't a field operative here? Unless…" Cody's gaze tracked to Garret.

"No, Garret isn't an operative. He's a civilian who got caught up in one of our missions."

"I'm a cop, not a civilian," Garret muttered.

"Listen," Betty said in her carefully honed doctor voice. She was gratified to see Cody stand a little straighter and shut his mouth. "Shay is hiding something. We think she's in trouble, but you know her. She's not going to let anyone else in on her trouble."

"What's the trouble?"

"We don't know. Elsie is still working on the specifics, but we know…someone threatened North Star. And she's acting like we neutralized that threat when we didn't. From what we've figured out, we think it's about her past. Do you know anything about Shay's life before North Star?"

Cody shook his head. "No. Why not go to Granger? He'd know."

Betty felt something uncomfortable twist in her stomach and she grimaced.

Cody blew out an irritated breath. "If you really think she's in trouble, you can't worry about her being angry you went to Granger."

"No, they're right to come here," Nina said, earning surprised looks from everyone. "I know a little something about Shay's past, and no, going to Granger wouldn't be the right answer. Not as a first step."

The carefully blank expression melted off Cody's face as he looked at his wife, registering sheer surprise. "You *know* something about Shay?"

Nina shrugged. "When you've been a woman on the run, you recognize the signs. I don't know what she was running away from, but whatever it was, she hid within North Star. She wasn't after revenge. She was looking to disappear."

Cody nodded thoughtfully. "I don't know about the hiding, but one thing is definitely true. It was never revenge for her. Not in the way it was for me." He scowled.

"If I had time to think, I could probably put some things together."

"We don't have a lot of time," Garret said. "She's planning something."

Betty looked back at Garret. "Why do you say that?"

"A woman like Shay, in charge of a big secret group? She's not waiting around, twiddling her thumbs like she's pretending to be doing. She's planning."

Cody and Nina nodded.

"Shay'd be patient if she had to be," Nina said, rubbing her belly. "But she wouldn't not act. She is *all* action. If her past is threatening North Star…"

Cody's frown deepened. "She'd sacrifice herself first." He swore, but then studied Betty and Elsie. "She also wouldn't expect you two to strike out on your own or go behind her back. It'd be a surprise if you two tried to stop her."

"Exactly," Betty returned.

He exchanged a look with his wife, and she nodded.

"I can help," he said. "I know you've got better computer skills than I do, Els, but if you're traveling, I've got better equipment. I've also got some information on some of the missions I did with Shay. Maybe we can unearth something."

Elsie nodded, but Betty reached out and grabbed her arm before she and Cody could hurry out of the kitchen.

"Nina." She looked at the woman, who was staring at her stomach, rubbing it carefully. She didn't know Nina that well personally, but she knew Nina and Shay had become close over the years. "You have to tell us everything."

Nina looked up, at Betty, then at Cody. "I promised I wouldn't."

"Nina," Cody said, clearly shocked his wife knew more than he did.

"She's in serious trouble. All of North Star might be. New and old." Betty didn't want to scare Nina, not when she was so close to having her baby. She didn't want to scare Cody, not when he'd purposefully left North Star behind.

But she needed them all to understand that in order to be safe, they needed to share everything.

"I don't know much, but I do know Shay's real name. It's Veronica. Shay's her last name."

"Veronica Shay," Betty and Elsie and Cody repeated, clearly all shocked the woman they'd known for so long went by her *last* name and they'd never suspected.

"And I don't think she was born around here. I think she and Granger met when he was an FBI agent in Chicago. So if you're looking into something from her past—I'd start with that name and that place."

Betty exchanged a look with Garret. She figured they were on the same page. "Elsie, you stay here and do all the research you can."

"Are you going to Chicago?" Elsie asked.

Garret shook his head. "The threat isn't in Chicago. I think we go back to headquarters." He turned to Betty.

She nodded. "We'll tail Shay. You find any information, you tell us. She moves, we'll tell you."

Elsie nodded. "Okay."

"Thanks for your help, Nina. Cody."

Cody frowned at them. "Look, my wife is nine months pregnant. I'm not leaving her side, but...my brothers could help. Tucker was with North Star briefly, too. If you need more eyes, more bodies. We'll help whatever way we can. For Shay."

Betty moved and gave him a quick hug, then Nina. She'd patched them both up, and now they both had built this sweet little life in small-town South Dakota.

She'd use them if she needed them to help Shay, but for now she wanted to see what she and Garret could do on their own.

## Chapter Nineteen

"Never dreamed I'd be driving back and forth through Wyoming and South Dakota," Garret grumbled on their drive *back* to headquarters.

Still, they'd gotten information on their trip. Maybe they could have sent one person, or used a telephone, for Pete's sake, but Garret was glad they'd traveled as a team. Were working as a team. They had a better chance of succeeding against someone as smart and accomplished as Shay if they worked together.

"You didn't know anything about that—her name? Where she's from?" Garret asked since Betty had been silent for most of the drive. Silent and worried.

Betty shook her head. "I always assumed she had connections to the Sons of the Badlands. Was from South Dakota. Like me. Like Cody and Granger and Holden and Reece. We all had connections. I don't know what to think of…her now."

"Well, until we know more there's not much *to* think."

Betty lapsed into another silence. Her face was pensive and occasionally she'd open her mouth, then shut it abruptly. Almost as if stopping herself. He didn't know if that was a North Star thing or a personal thing, but he figured he'd give her an avenue to tell him either way.

"You can tell me, you know. What you're thinking."

She blinked, then looked at him, as if not quite understanding his words. "I'm a pretty independent person."

She spoke in a careful, measured tone. It felt a bit too much like letting him down easy. So he kept his expression and voice bland. "Okay."

"I had to be," she said, somewhat fiercely.

There was more, Garret could tell. But she was working up the courage for it, so he'd give her the time. The way he saw it, they had time. So he reached over and put his hand over hers as he drove down the empty highway, the sun blazing into a riotous sunset around them.

Betty sighed. "We have more important things to focus on than how my past shaped me."

"Maybe, but we've also got a good half hour before we reach headquarters."

Betty looked out the window. "What we're going into is dangerous, and I have seen you work in dangerous situations a few times now. You're a martyr."

"I thought we were talking about you," Garret grumbled.

She smiled sadly and shook her head. "That's the thing. That *is* about me. What I've seen. What I've done. I grew up in that gang—but not. Dad protected me, but the men in that group weren't going to ignore his young, pretty daughter forever. He buried his head in the sand about that for a while, but when he couldn't, rather than get us both out, he got me out. Stayed there. Died there. He sacrificed himself for me."

"Maybe there wasn't a way to get you both out," Garret offered. He'd only known he was a father for a matter of weeks, only held his daughter for a day, really, and still he couldn't imagine *not* sacrificing everything he was for her. For Cain. If there was no other way, he'd sacrifice himself again and again.

Of course, he'd have done it long before any child of his understood what was happening, what kind of danger her everyday life was.

"Maybe," Betty said sadly. "But it always felt like *he* didn't know what he'd be if he got out, so he chose the punishment over the future." She turned to stare at him. He could feel her gaze, though he had to keep his eyes on the road.

"But you have to understand I let him. I knew what he was doing. I knew he would die if he stayed and I walked away when he gave me the opportunity. I didn't argue. I didn't beg him to come with me. I let him die like that, because it saved *me*."

"Am I supposed to be shocked and think you're a terrible person?"

"I did it to you, too. I left you there and—"

"And it turned out okay."

"It might not have."

"No, it might not have. That's a risk you take sometimes. I'd sacrifice myself for a lot of people, Betty. I can't lie and say I wouldn't. But I wouldn't sacrifice myself if there was another option. A better option, with a future and a life ahead of me. With my kids in it. With you in it. If there was no better option, I'd want you walking away, making something of your life. That'd be the *point* in the sacrifice."

"I'm so sick of sacrifice haunting me," she whispered.

He managed a quick glance, saw the tears in her eyes. Tears she never fully shed. He could only squeeze her hand and offer what little he could.

Because he didn't think she was done with other people's sacrifices just yet.

Betty cleared her throat. "I'm going to call and check on Savannah. She said the Vianni name. If she wakes up, maybe she can give us more."

Garret nodded as Betty got her phone out.

He didn't know Shay well enough to have any thoughts on what she might be hiding, but he thought about sacrifice. When you were a family—like Betty's father for her, and what he'd do for his own children—you'd put yourself in harm's way, again and again, to keep the ones you loved safe.

Shay had wanted everyone to keep them close. Safe.

Betty was talking in low tones on the phone, so he didn't interrupt her with his theory. He knew Elsie had set something up inside of headquarters to keep an eye on Shay, though both women had been against straight-up invading her privacy to spy on her. Just some kind of location tracker in case she left.

"She's still alive, but…they don't think she's strong enough to make it. Her organs are shutting down. She's had in-and-out moments, but none of them lucid."

Garret didn't know what to say to that. What to feel.

"I should have done more," Betty said in a whisper.

"What more could you have done?" Garret asked. He knew he couldn't get rid of her guilt. When you dealt in any kind of first response, guilt was par for the course. You just had to learn to cope with it.

"I don't know." Betty sighed.

Garret considered telling her about his theory on Shay sacrificing herself, but he picked up a flash of something in the rearview mirror. He watched the sedan follow them. When they got to the turnoff to headquarters, he purposefully didn't turn down it.

"Why are you going this way? Headquarters is—"

Garret kept his eyes on the rearview mirror. "We're being followed. Get the gun out of my bag."

BETTY WAS ALREADY emotionally wrung out. Feeling too many things all at once. So Garret's words didn't fully penetrate at first.

"Bet, sweetheart, you've got to get the gun out of my bag." He spoke to her like he needed to be *gentle*. "Carefully," he continued. "Try to keep it from looking like you're reaching for anything."

She inhaled and reminded herself that this was no different from a medical emergency. She had to stay calm and follow the steps. She reached for Garret's bag in the back seat, doing her best to keep her head faced forward.

"Oh, God, Garret," she said as terror gripped her. "We left Elsie behind with Cody and his fam—"

"No," Garret cut her off. "We didn't have the tail then. It didn't start until we got close to headquarters. They haven't been following us the whole time." He said it firmly. Assuredly.

She swallowed and figured it was best to believe him. "We should still warn them."

"We will. Gun first. Then you can send Elsie a text. If Shay is worried about a leak, and protecting the rest of us, we can't risk involving anyone else."

"Sabrina. I trust Sabrina."

"She's with that Connor guy, though, right?"

"He said the Vianni name." Betty carefully reached her arm back and felt around for Garret's bag. She had to twist a little to see where the zipper to the duffel was, but she made it look like she'd turned to talk to Garret. "Out loud to everyone. I can't imagine he's the leak."

Garret shook his head. "We can't go with an unknown. Do you think Shay really wants to think someone in her team is leaking information?"

Betty swallowed. No, Shay wouldn't want to believe it. It would be such a blow. Still, Betty couldn't bring herself to believe the people she knew and trusted could do something like this. Tear them apart. Put them in danger.

Her hand closed around the gun and she slowly pulled it out of the bag.

"Turn the safety off," Garret instructed. "Then hand it to me."

Betty did as she was told. But she kept hoping this was…overkill.

"Maybe it's Shay following us? If it started right before headquarters, maybe it's—"

"It isn't Shay, and it isn't North Star."

The way he said that had a cold shudder of fear moving through her.

"Put your head down, Betty."

"Garret—"

"Just keep your head low, okay? Don't give them the opportunity to shoot you."

"What about you?"

He didn't answer that. Just took the gun when she handed it to him, still steering with his free hand. His eyes moved from the rearview mirror and then the road in front of them with an ease that would have been impressive if she wasn't huddled low in the passenger side of the car scared half to death.

"Why is someone following us?"

Garret's eyebrows drew together as if thinking that over. "If it goes back to the beginning—the kids, and us all being at the airport... I was supposed to take the bait."

"But you aren't a part of North Star."

"No. But North Star has felt some kind of responsibility for me since the Nate mission. So I still work as bait. But they also knew you were taking care of me. If there's a leak, if they know enough about North Star to try to threaten it through me..." He shook his head in frustration. "I can't put the pieces together quite yet."

Betty couldn't, either. None of these disparate things made sense. "Cliff is in jail and Savannah is in the hospital..."

"I don't care what Shay said, they weren't the ringleaders. What was this Cliff guy waiting around for? The entire North Star team to go into that cabin? They should have acted, but they didn't. Because they were waiting on someone or something."

Betty thought back to that moment when Cliff had been in the room with her. Ready to hurt her in whatever ways he wanted. Wasn't that action?

But maybe not. Maybe it was *distr*action.

"Shay was afraid to send her men in," Garret was saying, still trying to fit those pieces together.

"I've never known Shay to be afraid to send a team in," Betty said. So many missions, and Shay had always trusted her team. Even when she was being careful with them.

"It was meant to be an ambush. She outsmarted it. But if she did…"

"She knew it was coming," Betty finished for him. "She knows what's coming."

"At least partially," Garret agreed. "If she knew everything, we wouldn't need to stay close. Where was she when she didn't come back for a while?"

"No one knows. So, she…was planning something?"

Garret shrugged a little, the speed increasing. Betty glanced in the rearview mirror. The car got no closer, its speed matching theirs. Not gaining on them, not shooting, just…following.

Betty considered what they'd experienced back in that cabin. "Cliff. He said he wanted to hurt North Star. Not kill them or anything. That's revenge."

"And revenge is personal." Garret spared her a brief look. "If someone was coming for Shay—for revenge against her personally—what would Shay do?"

"Whatever it took to prot…" Betty's heart sank like a stone. It was all so clear now. Hadn't they just been talking about sacrifice? "You think she's… Oh, *God*. I have to call her."

She expected Garret to argue, but he nodded. "See if you can talk some sense into her. She knows more than she's letting on, but she's also planning more than she's letting on. And my bet is on something that puts her in a lot more danger than she needs to be."

Betty swore, her shaky hands fumbling with her phone.

"If she doesn't answer, leave a message. Make sure to tell her someone is after us so she calls us back. Just keep your head low and hold on. Things are about to get bumpy."

With that, Garret took a sharp turn onto an unmarked gravel road that even Betty didn't know where it led.

But she'd trust Garret to keep them as safe as he could, and she'd call Shay and talk some sense into her.

*Please, let me talk some dang sense into her.*

SAVANNAH COULDN'T THINK STRAIGHT. Her thoughts swirled with pain and odd flashes of light. She heard beeps and murmured voices. Sometimes she could come to for a few moments, but the doctors or nurses always seemed to be talking about how long she'd last.

*Not much longer now.*

She was dying. Too much blood lost. Too much exposure to the elements. The doctor who'd worked on her in the helicopter had tried, but the damage had been done.

She was dying. She thought maybe there was another option here. She could fight, instead of lean into the obliterating darkness. But those flashes of light scared her. They felt like judgment more than that blankness she was looking for.

But the other option was to fight. Claw her way back to being alive. She managed to open her eyes, found the blinding light of the hospital room confronting enough to close them again.

Except she'd seen the flash of a face… Did she recognize that face? Would it be better to just let go and die?

She saw one of those flashes of light, that wasn't death. She didn't know what it was except she wanted nothing to do with it. So she opened her eyes.

The man was dressed in black. No doctor. No nurse.

"You know what I'm here for. Tell me everything Cliff found."

She didn't have the energy to laugh. Or flip him off. She could only stare at the man as he pulled a gun from inside his black jacket. "You don't tell me, you're dead."

Savannah thought that over. The way the doctors were talking, the way it felt like she was losing pieces of herself to a darkness too deep to be unconsciousness, she thought she was probably dead already.

She'd reached for the stars and come up empty. Better to die there than deal with the consequences of her actions.

"Who's Cliff?" she managed to croak.

He pointed the gun at her. As if she hadn't already been shot. As if some strange woman hadn't tried to save her. Tried and failed but tried all the same.

"You're just a pawn, Savannah. Pawns are disposable."

"I know." She'd always known that. And known that pawns didn't win in the end. But she found, in this strange haze of drugs and uncomfortable, twisting feelings over Betty and Garret both risking themselves to save her, she wasn't going to be the pawn in the end. "Go ahead and kill me, then. I'm not telling you anything."

If they wanted Veronica Shay and her secret group, then they could get her on their own.

# Chapter Twenty

Garret didn't know the area well enough to know where to drive. He had absolutely no plans to risk Betty, but he also needed to see what their tail would do if given the chance to approach.

This isolated gravel road seemed just the place.

Betty was talking, though it was clear she was leaving a message rather than actually getting through to Shay. Garret just kept following the gravel road. There was a dilapidated fence on one side, untamed fields on both. If anyone was farming or ranching the land, they weren't doing a very good job.

"Why aren't they *doing* anything?" Betty asked, peeking her head over the seat to look out the back window.

"Maybe they were searching for headquarters. Waiting for us to just lead them there." Garret considered the possibility.

"If there's a leak, wouldn't that person just tell them where headquarters is?" Betty returned. She was looking at her phone again, typing something—likely a text to Shay.

"Maybe we need to step back. Examine the individ-

ual threads. We have two theories, more or less. Some-
one from Shay's past before North Star is after her.
That doesn't match with Cliff wanting to hurt North
Star—"

"Unless the person knows how much North Star
means to Shay," Betty pointed out.

Garret grunted. Too many *ifs* and *unlesses*. But that
was how his life worked. A lot of questions he usually
had to find the answers to—wading through lies and
indifference and people's faulty memories.

He had to approach it like a case. "Okay, so that's
one hand—Shay's past. The other hand is Shay thinks
there's a leak *in* North Star that she's trying to figure
out on her own."

"How do we connect them?" Betty mused. "*Do* they
connect?"

They weren't going to figure that out driving around
with a tail. Or sitting here talking themselves to death.
Sometimes solving a case meant patience and waiting.

And sometimes it meant action.

Garret turned the car in a quick circle and then
jerked it to a stop, facing the car that had been following them. "Think about that while I take care of this.
Stay low."

Betty made a grab for his arm, but he maneuvered
out of her grasp, opening the door and using it as something like a shield between him and the other car. Just
in case. "There's only one person in the car. I can handle it. Trust me."

Betty swallowed audibly, but she nodded, big brown
eyes staring up at him. She didn't want to let him go,
but she trusted him. "Okay," she said, nodding slowly.

It meant something. Time and time again when one of them had to trust the other to handle something on their own, they did. They could. They had to.

Garret studied the car in front of him from behind the open car door. There could be more than the driver—hiding in the back—but he didn't get the impression this was a takedown mission.

Because this wasn't about him or even Betty. It was about Shay. Whether it was a leak or something from her past or even something they hadn't figured out yet, whatever was going on centered around Shay.

Garret slowly got to his full height and closed the door. He glanced back once to make sure Betty was keeping low. He saw no sign of her from the windshield, so that was good.

He turned all of his attention to the other car. The driver slowly got out, studying their surroundings, Garret, everything with obvious suspicion. Like Garret, he held a gun. Safety off, the business end pointed at the ground.

"Howdy, friend," Garret drawled, forcing a fake smile and a relaxed demeanor he didn't feel. "You seem to be a bit lost."

"You're not Granger Macmillan."

*That* took Garret off guard, but he tried to keep the easy smile on his face. "No, I'm not."

"And who's that?" the man asked, pointing the gun at the car.

Garret stepped into the man's sight line so that if he did indeed pull the trigger, it would be pointed at him, not Betty. "I think it's my turn to ask a question. Who are you?"

The man's eyes narrowed. He didn't lower the gun, but his finger wasn't wrapped around the trigger.

"You'll take me to Granger Macmillan," the man said. "Now. Or you die."

Garret didn't have to fake the smile. It came easily. "I don't even know who that is, friend."

"I'm not your friend. It seems like you're going to have to die, then."

Garret took a step forward, and then another, carefully watching the man's finger. As long as it didn't curl around the trigger, he could keep moving forward. "A lot of work to kill me over something you have to know I don't know anything about."

"I don't know who you are or what you know," the man returned. "But one of you knows how to get in touch with Granger Macmillan. One way or another."

Garret kept moving. Carefully. Slowly. Once close enough, he'd disarm the man and get the information he wanted. "I can assure you, I don't."

"What about her?" But he scowled before Garret could make up an answer. "All right. That's far enough," the man said when Garret had reached the halfway point between them. "I could just shoot you."

"You could," Garret agreed. "But I don't know who you are, and as far as I can tell, you don't know who I am. Seems a bit silly to kill a stranger. A *lot* of cleanup."

"I want Granger. Get her out of the car. Have her tell me she doesn't know how to get to him."

Since Garret knew full well Betty would be able to contact Granger Macmillan, he stalled and edged another step closer. He just needed a couple more feet and then he could take the man down.

He didn't look like much of a fighter. Too thin and narrow. Not muscle-bound.

The man stepped toward Garret now, pointing the gun right at him, his finger getting ready to move to that trigger. "I want Granger. You don't get me him—you die. And so does—"

Garret heard the car door behind him swing open, watched the man's eyes sweep toward the car, far behind him now. It was a split second of distraction, and Garret took it.

He lunged and hoped he wouldn't come up short.

BETTY SWALLOWED DOWN a scream when the gunshot went off and a loud *pop* followed by a hiss exploded not too far from her. As the car began to lean, she realized the bullet had hit their tire and *thankfully* not Garret.

Who was grappling with the man on the ground. The gun still in the man's hand. Clearly, Garret was trying to wrestle it away, but the man's narrow frame hid a wiry strength. Or perhaps just fight born of desperation.

Betty edged closer, trying to see if she could help in some way. She wasn't the best fighter, but she knew how to punch and kick. But they moved too fast, rolling over the ground, grunting and swearing and failing to dislodge from one another.

Where was Garret's gun? She looked around the grass where they were grappling. She saw the glint of metal and strode toward it. She picked it up, studied the make and model, then pointed it at the trees beyond.

When the shot rang out, both men startled to a stop. Now that they'd stilled, she pointed the gun at the man underneath Garret.

"Let go of your gun," Betty ordered the other man.

She watched him consider. Garret also had a grip on the gun, so clearly the man couldn't jerk it away and shoot like he wanted to. Eventually, he relented. Garret got up off him, pointing the man's gun at its owner.

The man on the ground had a look of disgust on his face. But he said nothing else. Made no threats or attempts to move. He just lay there.

"Thanks," Garret said to Betty. He was breathing heavily, and she could tell his shoulder was paining him. But she didn't have time right now to look at or rebandage the wound.

"Can you go grab my bag?" Garret asked. "I've got something I can tie him up with in the vest in there."

Betty nodded. She got him the supplies they needed and even though he was in pain, Garret tied the man up to his own satisfaction. Then he stood and stepped away.

"Let's head out. I'm sure someone will come for him."

"He shot out our tire."

"Then we'll take his car. Maybe we'll even find some useful information in it." Garret smiled down at the man. "I owe you one, buddy."

He sauntered over to the man's car and Betty trailed behind him, still holding Garret's bag. She didn't know what to think about this or how it fit into anything they'd previously thought.

"He wants Granger," Garret said in a low voice once they were out of earshot. "That's the guy you guys were talking about, right? The one who helps out North Star sometimes."

Betty frowned. "Yes, he's the old boss. He created

North Star. When he was injured, he had Shay take over. He never came back."

"Seems like maybe it's more about North Star than Shay, then."

"Seems like," Betty echoed, but it scraped along her nerves all wrong. A discordant note. An insistent feeling she should be able to figure this out. "He was always easier on Shay than anyone else."

"How do you mean?" Garret shook his head. "Hold that thought. Let's get to headquarters before whoever he's working for sends some backup." He got into the other man's car, and Betty had no choice but to get into the passenger seat.

The keys were in the ignition and Garret turned it over. "Nice ride," he murmured. He glanced into the back seat. "Jackpot. Look through this guy's things while I drive us back to headquarters."

Betty did as she was told, but her mind was racing. She was one of the few people still with North Star who'd been around since the beginning. Shay had already been in place as a field operative, as had a few other people now long gone back into civilian lives. But they hadn't run more than one mission when Granger had decided he needed a medic on staff.

Betty's phone vibrated in her pocket. She fumbled for it, hoping against hope it was Shay. Shay with answers and an explanation. So that this could be over instead of an unsolvable mystery.

But it was Elsie. Betty tried to hide her disappointment as she answered. "Els. Did you find anything?"

"Maybe," Elsie replied. "I found an odd kind of connection we didn't know about."

"Connection?"

"Well, we all know Granger's wife was killed by a Sons of the Badlands member, right?" Elsie asked, dragging the moment out—not purposefully but because she was typing something into her computer. Betty could hear the faint clacking of keys and could picture Elsie sitting in some uncomfortable position, nose to the screen, lost in the information she was unearthing.

"Yes, I think most people know that except maybe a few of the new recruits."

"Okay, yeah, I thought so. It's just… I found a Veronica who matches all the information I have on Shay. Except for the last name, but it fits. It all fits. Except… Or even more so because this Veronica was married to a guy by the name of Paul Vianni."

"Am I supposed to know who that is?" Betty asked, trying to find her patience, though it was straining. She kept looking through the man's things, phone cradled between chin and shoulder. Mostly there were just clothes, a book, a flashlight. Nothing at all to say who he was or what he was doing.

"Granger's wife's maiden name was Vianni. So Shay maybe had some connection to Granger's wife's family. Before North Star was even a thing. Back when they were all in Chicago. Together."

Betty didn't know how to respond to that. How to take it all on. It didn't make sense, but that man had been asking about Granger. And she *knew* Granger had Chicago connections from a mission that had gone wrong over two years ago now. The one that had taken Granger out of commission. The one that had involved the Viannis.

Could this have nothing to do with North Star at all?

But why were she and Garret involved? How was Savannah and Nate's mission connected? "None of this makes sense," Betty muttered. And she knew they were running out of time.

# Chapter Twenty-One

Garret drove back toward headquarters, watching for another tail, but none appeared. He kept thinking about what the man had said. *You're not Granger Macmillan.*

Why had the man thought he would be?

Betty ended her phone call with Elsie, a thoughtful frown creasing her brow. "Don't go to headquarters."

"Where should I go?"

"I'm not sure. Well…" Betty fell into silence, but it was clear she was arguing with herself about something. Garret let her think it over and didn't take the turnoff to North Star headquarters.

Of course, he didn't know the area that well, so all he could do was drive straight on the highway as the sun fully disappeared and night descended.

"Elsie found a connection between Shay and Granger that existed before North Star."

"That guy. He thought I'd be Granger. Then he wanted me to take him to Granger. I pretended I didn't know who he was, which was easy considering I barely know."

Betty nodded. "Maybe he's in trouble, too."

"Maybe he is the trouble," Garret pointed out.

"He *created* North Star. He…hired me. Granger Macmillan is the reason the Sons of the Badlands no longer exists."

Granger nodded along as Betty recounted all the things this Granger had done. "Then he left, right?"

"You don't understand. He was shot, and our original headquarters was bombed. He was badly injured. He physically couldn't be our leader for a while. But…" She trailed off again, frowning into the dark outside her window.

"Bet?"

"I'm sorry. I'm just trying to make sense of it all. I'm trying to think logically and without emotion. Anyone can be bad. I know that."

"But?"

"But Shay and Granger *aren't*. I know them. They're…family. Granger recruited me. Shay has been my closest friend for almost a decade. They couldn't just…hide all that bad from me."

"I was married to Savannah for a year. I thought I knew her, too." It settled like an acidic weight in his gut. A failure. And he couldn't even regret it anymore because it had brought him Cain and Maggie.

"That was different," Betty insisted. "She was purposefully tricking *you*. For a purpose. Maybe right now Shay and Granger are covering something up, but it wasn't always that way. It isn't their endgame." She looked at him as he drove down the dark, deserted highway. "We have to figure out the endgame. I think… I think I need to go see Granger."

"You didn't want to before."

"I know. I still don't want to. But maybe he doesn't know what's going on. Maybe he could help Shay."

"And if it makes everything worse?"

Betty blew out a breath. "At this point? What are our other options? Wait?"

Though it pained him, Garret shrugged. "We could."

"You want to get home with your babies, Garret. And you deserve that."

He slid a look at her. "Is that what you want, Bet?"

She kept her gaze on the dark outside the windshield, but she seemed to be thinking. "Yes, selfishly, yes. I'm…tired of all this. Questions without answers. Running here and there to sew everyone up. I want a piece of what Reece and Cody found. I think I deserve it, and so do Granger and Shay." She finally turned to look at him. "Whatever is going on with them, they're trying to protect us. Those of us who have connections to North Star. I know that deep in my heart. I'd bet everything I am on it. Even my life. But if you don't—"

Garret reached out and laid his hand on her knee. "If you're laying down your life, Bet, I'm there."

She blew out a breath, then leaned her head on his shoulder. "Keep driving until we get to the four-way stop. Then you'll take a right. We've got about an hour of driving ahead of us."

"Got it."

So, he drove, Betty's head on his shoulder. He didn't know the players as well as she did, so he had to trust her, but… "I keep going back to my involvement. I know that sounds self-involved, but…why am I here?

I don't connect to any of this. *Except* Nate's mission. Somehow, this connects to what went on with Nate."

"Nate's mission was just about Courtney using him, while she tried to screw over her jerk of a grandfather."

"But underneath what Courtney was using Nate for was what Nate actually uncovered when he was in the Navy. He found illegal arms deals by his commander. Where were those weapons going?"

"Shay handled all that. Elsie would know. A few other operatives. I'm sure I heard the information, but wouldn't have paid much attention. Missions aren't my job."

"Text Elsie to add that to her list of information we want. If we get to this Granger guy and he won't fill in the gaps, we'll fill them in ourselves."

Betty tapped away on her phone as Garret drove, following the directions she'd given him. They had a long way to go yet, and the world outside the car sparkled in moon and starlight.

"Oh, my God," Betty breathed, looking at something on her phone. "Mallory just texted me…" She looked up at him. "Savannah's dead." Betty's voice shook as she relayed the information. "Not because of the coma. Someone snuck into her hospital room and killed her."

Garret didn't know what washed over him. A tangled mix of emotion, regret being a significant thread. That Savannah had made the choices she had. That someday he'd have to endeavor to explain all this to their children.

He'd failed to protect— He shook that thought away. This wasn't about him. That was the mistake he'd made with Nate. Making everything about himself and what he'd believed of his brother or hadn't.

Savannah had made her choices, and Garret had to accept that there was nothing he could have done to change them. He could feel…disappointed that she'd made them. Regretful that they'd ended up killing her.

But it wasn't about *him*.

He glanced at Betty. Her face was pale, and even though the moonlight and streetlights were the only thing illuminating her face, he could tell she was paler than she should be. He reached over and put his hand on her leg. "You did what you could."

Betty swallowed. "But it wasn't enough."

"Sometimes you can't save people, Betty. Especially when they choose a road like the one Savannah did."

She turned to face him. "You're trying to tell me you won't feel guilty?"

He blew out a breath, watching the road as he drove. "I don't know what I'll feel. I don't know what I feel now. But what I do know, at the core of everything, is Savannah made her choices. I couldn't stop them. For a long time I blamed myself for that. Long before I understood what she was a part of. But if there's anything that Nate's whole mission taught me, it's that you can only control yourself, take responsibility for yourself. Everyone is going to make their own choices. Sometimes they're wrong, sure, and maybe there will be guilt over that. But we got her out, Bet. We did what we could for her. I can feel…remorse and regret without feeling like there was anything else I could have done."

Betty squeezed her eyes shut. "I can't… We have to

get to Granger and get to the bottom of this." But she laced her fingers with his. A connection. A comfort.

A *partnership*.

He lifted her hand to his mouth and pressed a kiss to the back of her hand. "We will."

BETTY HAD TRIED to sleep, but her brain was too full of…everything. Regret and blame and frustration and worry. Grief, maybe, though it felt silly to mourn a woman she barely knew.

But that woman had risked her life to keep Betty from something terrible. She'd died because…

Well, because of what she'd been involved in. Because of the choices she'd made. And because some people out there were straight-up evil.

It wasn't fair, but life wasn't fair. And Savannah's children would have to know that, probably at far too young an age.

*Just like you did.*

So maybe she had something to offer those babies. Something Garret couldn't. He'd had a good, stable family growing up in a nice small town. Sure, he'd seen things as a cop and learned hard lessons later in life, but she could be the one who understood what it was like to feel conflicted over a parent. And what their subsequent disappearance from a family felt like.

She couldn't do anything else for Savannah now. Dead and gone. But she could give her this.

Garret squeezed her hand as they came to the last turnoff. Just a few miles down the road they'd get to Granger's ranch.

Dread filled her. "What if this doesn't work?"

"We'll see what Elsie's got and figure out a next step." He slowed to a stop in front of a ramshackle house. There were no lights on inside, but two dogs came trotting up to their car and sniffed around it— sounding no alarms. Betty knew their names were Mays and Ripken, and likely they knew her scent. She sure hoped they did anyway.

"I promise you, Bet, I'm not stopping until this is figured out. For my kids. For you. We'll just keep going until we get it sorted. That's all you can do sometimes."

She leaned over the console, struck by...everything about him. She pressed her mouth to his. Quick, but gentle. "Thank you," she said earnestly.

"It's not a thing to thank me for. It's just—"

She placed her hand over his mouth. "Thank you just the same," she said firmly. Before she could say anything else or get out of the car, her phone lit up. Shay's code name popped up on the screen.

Betty grabbed it, too quickly, fumbling with the right buttons to push. "Shay?"

"Where are you, Betty?" She sounded tired. Worn down to the bone. Betty could think of maybe one time when she'd heard that tone from Shay.

It had been after the explosion, when they weren't sure Granger was going to make it.

That didn't bode well.

Betty slid a glance at Garret, then at the dark house haloed in moonlight in front of her. She'd never lied to Shay. Ever since she'd been free of her old life, she'd made promises to herself about the kind of person she was going to be. She could fib a bit for the greater good, but...

Well, wasn't this the greater good?

"Garret didn't want to stay put. I thought it best not to let him go off on his own."

"And Elsie?"

"What about Elsie?"

There was a long, heavy silence. "I don't know what you're all trying to do, but it's making my life harder."

Betty's heart twisted. "How, Shay?"

"Just convince Garret to come back, huh? It can't be good for you guys driving those babies around all night. All of you come on back and we'll go from there."

So Shay didn't know they'd dropped the babies off, or left Elsie with Cody and his computer equipment. Obviously Betty had asked Reece and Cody and Nina not to say anything, but she hadn't been sure their loyalty would be to her over Shay.

"Are you at headquarters?" Betty asked.

Another long pause from Shay. Betty closed her eyes.

"Shay, I don't know what's going on, but whatever it is, doing it alone isn't an option. So I can't come back. We can't come back. Not until you let us in. We know these people after North Star want you in particular." She considered before she added the second part. "And Granger."

There was the faintest sound of an intake of breath, but that was it. "Granger doesn't have anything to do with this. And you're overreacting. I'm not doing anything on my own. Or I wouldn't be if my head tech operative hadn't taken off."

It was a lie. Betty only knew because if it were true, Shay would have already put Elsie on the case before they left.

"Would you all please just come back so we can get to the bottom of this?" Shay asked, and there was *something* in her voice. Betty knew she was lying. She was just trying to get them back. But there was an... exhaustion underneath it all.

Guilt twisted, but Garret was right. People made their choices, and until Shay made the choice to let them help, Betty couldn't be swayed by exhaustion. "The bottom of what?"

Betty could practically *see* Shay scowling. "We got the main players, but we don't know the *whys*. That's all."

Betty thought about that. Garret had said Cliff and Savannah couldn't be the main players because they'd been waiting around—and he'd been right about that. Betty didn't want to believe Shay was flat-out lying to her, but what else was there to believe?

"I'm sorry, Shay. Until you're ready to really tell Elsie or me the truth, we aren't coming back."

"I am your superior, Betty. If you don't come back..."

"You're going to kick me out of North Star?"

"Maybe I will," Shay returned, a rare snap to her voice.

Betty might have been hurt, but mostly she was just scared for her friend. And determined to see this through. "Then you'll have to kick me out. Goodbye, Shay." She ended the phone call and let out a long, slow breath.

"We'll get to the bottom of it," Garret assured her.

"She's scared. That's what I can't get over. Shay is *scared*, and she won't ask for help."

"Maybe she doesn't know how."

Betty studied Granger's dark house. Garret was probably right. A mix of not knowing how and wanting to protect people. She understood Shay's reasoning. But she couldn't abide by it. "Let's go."

## Chapter Twenty-Two

Garret stepped out of the car. The dogs were on Betty's side, sniffing and turning in excited circles. They jumped on her and she whispered greetings.

"What is it with you and dogs?" Garret muttered, missing Barney back at home. Missing *home* and just a normal life.

With Betty in it. And his babies.

He'd do whatever it took to get there.

"Dogs love me," Betty said, and he could see the hint of a smile in the moonlight. Which was much better than the despair he'd seen on her face as she'd talked to Shay on the phone.

He walked over to her, the dogs now sniffing him suspiciously. Betty took his hand in hers and the dogs' tails began to wag. They all walked toward the cabin. The lights remained off, but Garret had the feeling they were being watched.

Betty walked right up onto the porch. Garret kept his free hand on the butt of his weapon, watching the inky black around them.

Betty, with absolutely no fear or worry, banged on

the front door. Minutes ticked by. Slow, tense minutes. But Betty didn't give up. She simply banged again.

A light popped on through the window and finally the door squeaked open. A bearded man in sweats opened the door with a glare on his face. "It's the middle of the night," he growled.

"Sorry to interrupt your beauty sleep," Betty returned brightly. "Consider this a house call and let us in."

Granger studied Betty, then Garret, then grunted in disgust and moved out of the doorway.

Betty stepped inside and Garret followed. They entered a small, dilapidated kitchen. Aside from electricity powering the lights and stove, it seemed a bit like the man was living far off the grid.

Granger moved over to the stove and an ancient stovetop coffeepot and began preparing coffee. "I was asleep, Betty."

But there was an alertness to him that made Garret not fully believe the man. Garret remained silent, though.

"Granger Macmillan, this is Garret Averly," Betty said, ignoring the sleep comment and the unwelcoming waves coming off the man. "Garret, this is Granger. He used to be head of North Star."

There was something about the way the man's shoulders tensed that made Garret wonder if *used to be* was something Granger felt comfortable with.

Once the coffee prep was complete and he was waiting for it to boil, he turned to face both of them. His expression was shrewd and careful. "Why are you here?"

"Why do you think I'm here?"

Granger rolled his eyes. "When have I ever been in the mood for your playing at psychiatrist, Bet?"

"When have I ever been in the mood for your non-answers, Granger? I gave you and North Star ten years of my life. I've patched you all up. Kept that group *running*, and the lot of you out of a pile of trouble and questions you would have otherwise faced."

"You helped us to do some good in the world."

"I did," Betty agreed.

Garret could see the doctor in her. That cool, calm and in-charge woman she'd been when stitching him up in his own cabin. Who'd artfully maneuvered him into healing, while making his dog fall in love with her.

She might not be some North Star field operative, but he could tell she was right. She was the heartbeat of that group, keeping it going for as long as it had, doing the good it had done.

She crossed her arms over her chest. "You owe me some answers."

Granger studied her for a long time.

"You said so yourself, Granger. I saved your life. You owe me."

Garret watched the exchange with some interest. Betty didn't seem like the type to use her position as doctor or saving people to get what she wanted, but clearly she was willing to pull out all the stops here.

"Follow me," Granger grumbled, pushing off the stove. He led them deeper into the house, flipping on lights as he went.

He led them into a room that Garret supposed was used as some kind of office. There was a big board hung on the wall. Papers, pictures, notes were tacked to it. An investigation board, like the detectives back at county used when they were trying to solve a particularly difficult case.

A lot of it was written in a kind of shorthand Garret couldn't decipher. Which he supposed was the point.

"I imagine you're trying to figure out what went down. I heard Savannah Loren died." He slid a glance at Garret. "Condolences."

Garret didn't know what to say to that. So he didn't reply. He watched Betty. She studied the papers. He wasn't sure she understood them any better than he did, but she pulled a picture off the board. It was of Shay, Elsie and Betty at the airfield when this had all started. Garret noted the airplane was in the picture—before it had exploded.

"Does Shay know about this?" Betty asked, wagging the photo at him.

"No."

She looked at Granger, a faint accusatory shift to her eyebrows. "Do you know about what happened in the cabin in Montana?"

Granger shrugged. "Some."

Betty blinked, and he could see she was coming to the same conclusion Garret had.

"Someone's leaking *you* information," she said.

Granger scowled. "I *invented* North Star. There are no *leaks* to me."

"You left North Star." There was accusation in Betty's tone, more even than in her expression. An old hurt, Garret supposed. He didn't know the circumstances, but he figured it was why Betty and Elsie had been reluctant to come to him in the first place.

"It was for the best."

"And now?"

"Betty, don't take this the wrong way. You're the doctor. I don't know why you got in the middle of this." This time when he looked at Garret it was as if to blame him. Though Garret had hardly brought *any* of this on Betty or even himself. He'd gotten involved with North Star simply to help his brother. "Go back to headquarters."

"And do what?"

"What do you mean? Do your job. Fulfill your role." Again Granger's gaze tracked to Garret. "And send this guy home."

"This guy will decide what he does, thanks," Garret replied. He knew Betty and the entire North Star crew cared about Granger. There was an odd kind of hushed awe when people talked about him. Garret had expected to find some kind of god.

Instead he saw a tired man who'd holed himself away from life. Garret looked at the board again. Someone inside was giving Granger the information to help, though.

*Vianni.* There was the name Elsie had told Betty about.

So, Granger knew it all connected, too.

"This guy got dragged into all of this against his will," Betty said, fighting back her temper. "At first I thought it was an accident. A man trying to help his brother. Now I think North Star made mistakes. One after the other—because you and Shay are keeping something from *everyone*."

Granger's expression didn't change. That blank-faced look she had once known so well. She'd even understood. A leader had to keep their emotions under control. When you were making life-and-death decisions, you had to leave emotions out of it.

He'd taught her that, and it had helped her become a better doctor.

But he wasn't a leader anymore. Certainly not hers.

"Don't worry about Shay. Shay can take care of herself."

"I suppose her being able to take care of herself is why you have all this?" Betty returned, pointing to the board. She noticed Garret had surreptitiously pulled off one of the smaller pieces of paper and slid it into his pocket.

She immediately looked past it so Granger wouldn't notice.

"Look. I'll handle it."

*Handle it.* That was rich, and then and there she decided she'd go ahead and let her temper take hold. Why not? This might be life-or-death, but she was tired of other people playing that game.

"You haven't handled anything since you left. You get dragged back into a mission here or there, kicking and screaming, to do something for us. But you always make Shay and anyone else feel terrible about it. We let you have your little tantrum. Well, I for one am done. You left. You abandoned us. And you gave Shay a garbage hill to climb in the process. You're not my superior anymore, Granger. I don't owe you anything."

His expression was blank, his hands in his pockets. She remembered, vividly, a few years ago being in a room with him while Shay went off on him about his choices. About putting his end goal above innocent people's safety.

He hadn't acted affected. Hadn't changed his stance. But Betty had noticed then and now the subtle bunching of hands into fists deep in his pockets.

"Who are the Viannis?" Garret asked, breaking the tense silence.

Granger's eyes widened a fraction, but then he gave a careless shrug. "The Viannis are an old mafia family. We broke them up a few years back, but there's a new faction involved in this whole military weapons mess. I guess they want revenge against North Star."

"Not just North Star. You and Shay in particular."

Granger's gaze was sharp and careful. "Maybe," he agreed, but it was too easy. Like he was giving a crumb to hide the whole.

Betty could do the same, but she thought showing her hand was the only way to get anywhere. "Your wife was connected to them. So was Shay."

For the first time, Betty saw a little crack. A flash of surprise, maybe even of worry. "Who told you that?"

"Elsie figured it out."

"Hell," Granger muttered. "Girl's sharp."

"That *woman*," Betty corrected, "got information you and Shay have hidden from all of us."

"We all hide our pasts, Betty. You should know that as well as anyone."

"I never hid my past."

"You didn't sit around talking about it with everyone, either, did you?"

"You knew." She met his gaze until he looked away.

Clearly she was at least kind of getting through that thick skull of his.

"I knew everyone's past, Betty. I was the person who recruited everyone…back then." He frowned a little. "This Lindstrom character."

Garret had also questioned Connor, and Betty knew she couldn't let her personal feelings cloud facts. Connor was new. He hadn't been recruited the way the rest of them had. He'd joined North Star because he'd fallen in love with Sabrina on a mission.

But that was why Betty couldn't believe Connor would be giving information to someone who would hurt them. She'd watched them together. The way Connor tried to protect Sabrina without her knowing that was what he was doing. The way he *looked* at her when he didn't think anyone was paying attention.

It couldn't be Connor. "Connor is honest to a fault. And would do anything—including leave his old, perfectly happy life behind—for Sabrina. Beyond that, if Connor was up to something fishy, Sabrina would know."

"She's injured."

"She'd know, Granger. You trained her yourself. You know she'd have figured it out."

Granger scowled.

"If we think there's a leak beyond someone giving Granger information," Garret said, his eyes studying the board like he could decipher Granger's complicated code, "maybe it doesn't have to be a specific person. Remember during Nate's mission?" He looked back at Betty. "Elsie found a computer thing she'd only heard of as gossip that tracked her stuff or whatever. Maybe it's a tech thing. In the computers or phones or some-thing? Maybe someone's getting information through the computers, not through the people."

"I'm not on any of the North Star communication systems," Granger said flatly. Flatly enough Betty won-dered if he was lying.

"You wouldn't have to be," Garret returned. "Only the person leaking you information from the inside would have to be."

He was right. Betty knew she was grabbing on to this theory because it meant everyone at North Star was innocent—except whoever had leaked info to Granger. Daniels, if she had to guess. But it was also just a solid theory. One to look into.

"I'll text Elsie. Maybe if she's aware, she'll notice something."

Granger clenched his jaw. "Look. Let me—"

"No. No one's handling this on their own. Not any-more." Too many factions, Betty realized. Too many people working against each other—all in the name of helping each other, sure. Protecting each other from having to talk about all the traumatic pasts that had brought them to a secret group. Hard life histories they'd all been willing to erase.

Betty sent the text to Elsie. Not just about the pos-sibility of a tech leak, but an instruction to come back. "We're all going to headquarters. And we're getting to the bottom of this once and for all. Together."

## Chapter Twenty-Three

Garret knew smiling wasn't appropriate in this situation, but he was rather enjoying watching tiny Betty order around the big, gruff, irritated Granger Macmillan. She told him what to pack, how fast to do it, then ordered him into the back seat of their car with his two dogs.

It was a packed car now, and the hour-long drive back to headquarters would take them toward early morning. But Betty was right. This had to be done as a team. They'd worked together—different factions, North Star and Averlys—all to get Nate out of the trouble he'd been in. Now it was time to get North Star out of whatever trouble they were in.

They'd been driving awhile in silence when Betty's phone chimed, and she looked at the text.

"Elsie said she's on her way. She thought she might have noticed something off about the computers, but they were having some problems with the comm units. She wants to check those out, but she'll need to be at headquarters to do it. Tucker Wyatt is coming with her."

Granger grunted in the back seat. "I thought I was done with Wyatts."

"I'm sure you told yourself you were done with a great many things," Betty returned primly. "Yet you took your hermit loner act only an hour away, and keep popping up during North Star missions. So *done* with everything," she said sarcastically.

Garret bit back a snicker.

"Even if Elsie can figure out what's been tampered with—saying it has been—that doesn't give us answers."

"So maybe you could," Garret returned. He might not know Granger that well, but he certainly knew the man was keeping some things to himself. Things Garret was pretty sure would help Betty figure out what was going on.

"I told you guys. This new faction of the Viannis is part of the weapons thing North Star has been trying to dismantle for the past few months. Every time we take one player down, another player pops back up. This time it was the Vianni family."

"A family you and Shay have ties to," Betty said.

"Far as I know, that's a coincidence. Every time they've connected to North Star, it's been...a coincidence."

But Garret didn't believe in coincidences. Not anymore. "How does Savannah connect to all this?"

Granger was silent for a long minute, petting his dogs in the back seat and watching the darkened landscape pass around them. "Look, I don't have all the answers. I'm just peripheral. I've got bits and pieces."

"That board was a hell of a lot more than bits and pieces."

"He deserves to know, Granger."

Granger sighed. "As far as I can tell, Savannah was

involved with the Loren arm of it, obviously. Her grandfather would smuggle the weapons from the military
and Savannah and her cousin Courtney, who you guys
took down last month, worked together to help deliver
weapons or collect payment or information. I'm only
guessing here, but I imagine Savannah's role in that was
supplying to or collecting from the Viannis. Then she
got mixed up with whatever they're doing."

Garret slid a look to Betty. She was thinking it over,
but it was clear she more or less believed what Granger
was saying.

"So why'd she end up dead, then?" Garret asked.

"Shay sent Gabriel and Mallory to the hospital to
figure that out."

Betty twisted in her seat to frown back at Granger.
"Gabriel *and* Mallory?"

"Sure. Pairs are better."

"It leaves fewer people at headquarters, though,"
Betty said. "I don't like that. I don't—"

"Slow down," Granger murmured from the back seat.

Garret glanced at Betty. She nodded, so they slowed.

"Look there," Granger said, pointing out the window.
On the side of the highway in the dim light of barely
dawn, Garret could make out tire ruts. Fresh ones.

"That's the second set I've seen," Granger said. "And
those aren't random trucks or farm vehicles." Granger
studied the area. "Someone knows where headquarters
is."

"They're surrounding it," Garret finished for
Granger. "At least three vehicles."

"If there's three on this side, I imagine there are
three on the other side of the turnoff. There's no way

in on the other side. Too wooded." Granger surveyed the woods around them.

"But headquarters has all sorts of security features," Betty said.

"But if someone could tamper with the comm units, someone could tamper with the security systems. Whoever this is, whatever threat we're dealing with, they've been patient and careful. I don't think they're moving on headquarters without knowing they can get through the security measures," Granger said.

Betty took a sharp intake of breath. "She's alone." Her head whipped to look at Garret with fear all over her expression. "She… When we wouldn't come back, I bet she sent everyone away. Gabriel and Mallory didn't need to go to Montana together. She did this on purpose so she could handle it alone," Betty said, sounding shocked to her core.

Garret wasn't shocked in the least. His mind was too busy zooming ahead. If Shay was surrounded, perhaps this group surrounding her wouldn't expect backup. But they might watch for it just the same.

"She couldn't have sent away Sabrina," Granger said, sounding concerned for once rather than cagey. "Not with her injuries. There'd be no excuse good enough."

Betty shook her head. "Sabrina has an appointment with a specialist in Casper tomorrow. All Shay had to do was encourage Connor to take her out there a day early. Everyone else she could have sent on missions or breaks or anything else. In fact, Elsie and I leaving gave her the perfect opportunity." Betty swore.

"It isn't your fault," Granger and Garret said practically in unison.

Betty opened her mouth, then shut it, shaking her head. "What are we going to do?"

Garret studied the area around them. They were coming up on the turnoff to headquarters. It was a good two miles off the highway.

"Any back ways in?"

"No," Granger said firmly.

"That isn't exactly true," Betty replied. She glanced at Granger. "She didn't tell you?"

Granger crossed his arms and sat back in the seat. "Nothing to tell. I wasn't part of North Star when you guys built this place."

But there was a tension there. A personal one they probably didn't have time for. He followed Betty's directions to a turnoff that was nearly invisible, and then a few more roundabout dirt roads someone would really have to know.

"We can't get any closer without detection from security measures if they're up," Betty said.

Garret pulled the car to a stop, wedging it as well as he could between a rocky outcropping and a tree and some brush.

Granger leaned forward in his seat, so his head appeared between him and Betty. "You're a cop, right?"

Garret nodded.

"We'll move in. Carefully. The goal is to get into headquarters without anyone seeing us—those cars and however many men they had, or Shay. She sees us, she can lock us out. Stealth is the name of the game, not speed. Likely the security measures are compromised, but maybe not all."

Granger started gathering what he'd brought and

slipped out of the car into the slowly breaking dawn outside. Garret got out of the car, too. He didn't have a bag of stuff, but he did have his gun and the vest Shay had given him back in Montana. They met at the front of the car, looking out over the broad clearing they would have to make it through undetected to get to headquarters.

"Know where you are?"

"Sort of."

Granger pulled out a phone and handed it to him. The screen had a map on it. "I'm not going to mark anything just in case, but we're here." He pointed to the lower left corner. "We want to meet here. So I'll take this route, and you'll take this one. Stay as protected as you can."

Garret nodded and tried handing the phone back to Granger, but Granger shook his head. He pulled another one out of his pocket. "Got backup. You take that one. Destroy it if things get bad, eh?"

"Are you forgetting something?" Betty demanded. She'd gotten out of the car and was standing in the middle of the rocky outcropping and tree with her arms crossed over her chest.

"You stay here," Granger and Garret said in unison.

Betty gave them each a long, cold stare. "Give me a gun, boys. I know how to shoot." She arched an eyebrow at Granger. "You taught me yourself."

"Yeah, and no offense, Bet, but you were my worst student." He gestured back at the car. "Someone has to stay with the dogs."

"I'll need a gun to protect the dogs," Betty replied, undeterred.

Granger muttered under his breath, then shrugged off his pack. He pulled out a handgun and stalked over to Betty before slapping it into her hand. "Stay out of sight. Protect yourself. We may need your medical expertise, so don't go getting shot before you can give it. Understood? Keep your phone on, we'll call if we need you. The gun is a *last* resort."

Betty took the sidearm, and Garret watched as she lifted her chin. She didn't agree with anything Granger said, but he was too busy making preparations and shrugging his bag back on.

Granger looked around the clearing. "You head west. I'll head east. If you get caught…"

"Fight like hell?" Garret offered.

Granger let out a soft laugh. "Yeah. That's about it." He took off walking east and Garret took a few steps west until Granger was out of sight. Then he turned to Betty, who was standing outside the car, the dogs on either side of her.

Garret sighed. "Come on."

Betty's eyebrows rose. "Where?"

"I'm not leaving you behind to wreak havoc. If you're determined to do this, we're at least going to do it together." He looked at the dogs. "They're likely trained?"

"Likely."

Garret figured he might regret it, but Betty had been right back at Granger's cabin. Whatever was happening could only be gotten through together. No lone sacrifices. No isolated attempts at bravery.

A bunch of smart, trained people working together to take down a threat. "Let's go."

BETTY COULD ADMIT Garret had surprised her. She'd expected to have to follow him quietly from a distance and hope he didn't see her, and that had been a debate in her mind because obviously she couldn't just leave Mays and Ripken behind.

Then he'd just told her to come along. "Well, I guess I don't have you completely pegged yet, Garret."

He smiled at her as they moved into the clearing. His eyes surveyed the landscape around them. He held his gun in one hand, loose and ready. She tried to mirror the movement. Though, unlike Elsie, who was excellent when not under pressure, Betty had *no* skill with guns—pressure or not. She knew how to use it, but something happened between the aiming and shooting that left her perennially very off course.

"First instinct was to have you stay back, but isn't that why we're in this mess? Everyone trying to take care of things on their own?"

Betty nodded, and that gave her an idea. "Can we make a quick call?"

Garret studied their surroundings. "Stay right here. Call whoever you need to. I'll leave one dog with you and take one with me if he'll go. I'm just going to make it to that ridge over there and see how far I can see beyond. When you're done and I'm satisfied, I'll wave you over."

"Okay." She watched Garret whisper commands to the dogs. Betty held Ripken's collar so he'd stay with her, while Garret patted his leg and waved Mays along to follow him.

Betty got out her phone. Instead of a call, she prepared to make a mass text. She had one Wyatt brother on the way with Elsie. They should arrive soon. She couldn't ask Cody to come, too, what with Nina being so close to going into labor. She didn't know the other ones.

She wouldn't ask Reece to break his retirement, if only because he was keeping Garret's babies safe. She considered Connor, off in Casper, then decided against calling on him. Sabrina would insist on coming and she just wasn't healed enough to be part of this.

Her best option was Holden, a former operative who would come without hesitation since he was only semiretired. She could call Gabriel and Mallory back—whatever had happened to Savannah could be investigated later. They couldn't have gone too far. It simply hadn't been long enough.

So, Betty texted Holden, Gabriel and Mallory and did her best to be informative but succinct.

All hands on deck. HQ surrounded. Approach with caution. Shay alone inside. DON'T USE COMM UNITS.

Betty knew it was possible their phones had been tapped or something, but it was a chance she had to take. Elsie had been more concerned about the comm units than the phones.

She glanced at Garret. He was waving her over so she hit Send and shoved her phone into her pocket. Ideally, backup would come and help, but she still had men on the ground now. Granger and Garret. She had to believe in their skills, just to keep her own sanity.

She moved across the clearing carefully, trying to be as watchful as Garret had been. When she was still a few yards away, Garret made a frantic sweep of his arms.

"Down," Garret ordered in a sharp hiss. Betty immediately fell to the ground, Ripken dropping onto his belly at the same time.

"Good dog," she whispered, wrapping her arm around the dog and pulling him close. She looked up to see Garret on the ground, too, army-crawling toward her. Mays lay down behind the rock cropping, alert but holding still at Garret's command.

Once Garret got close enough to whisper, he reached out and grabbed her hand. "I don't think we were spotted, but it was close. Crawl over here. I saw two. We're going to have to work together to try to pick them off."

Betty nodded and then they all crawled together to the rock cropping that would hide them from view and provide some protection from bullets.

Garret murmured low orders to the dogs. When Betty peeked over the top of the rocks, she could see two men moving slowly toward them, guns drawn.

"They're wearing vests," Garret said in her ear. "So we want to aim for arms, legs. Something that will debilitate them so I can go down and tie them up or what have you."

"Garret, I'm a terrible shot. Truly. I'd be as liable to hit the tree over there as an arm or a leg."

Garret nodded. He covered her hand with his, guiding her to wrap her hand around the gun. He positioned her gun, resting it on the outcropping. Then he positioned her wrist, her hand. "All you have to do is stay really still and pull the trigger when I say *go*. Okay?"

Betty nodded. Nerves threatened to make her hand shake, but she was a doctor who'd dealt with much worse. She'd stitched up thrashing men in the middle of the Badlands. Been dropped into blizzards to set broken bones and dig bullets out of men's arteries.

She could hold a damn gun still.

"On the count of three, and then *go*. Breathe in and out. Stay steady," Garret ordered in calm, low tones. He positioned himself much like he'd positioned her.

The sound of a gun exploding had Betty jerking in surprise, but she didn't make a noise. As far as she could tell it hadn't landed anywhere near them. The dogs startled, but both she and Garret used their free hands to calm them.

Garret reached over and repositioned her arm and gun.

"One…" Garret whispered, taking in a slow breath. He exhaled *two*. She followed his breathing pattern. On *three* she did her best to focus, aim and shoot.

"Go."

She'd braced herself for the noise of the gunshot, but it still jolted her, reverberating in her ears. Garret pulled her hand down and shot once more, before ducking behind the rocky outcropping.

"You were supposed to take the guy on the left."

"I was *aiming* for the guy on the left's left arm."

"Good Lord. You hit the one on the right's right ankle, Bet," Garret muttered. "Avoid shooting from here on out if you can. Stay here with the dogs. I'm going to tie them up. Keep an eye on me and… I was going to say shoot if someone appears, but just…yell or something."

She opened her mouth to argue with him, but he was gone, and she had to grab Mays's collar to keep him from taking off after Garret. Once the dogs were settled, she carefully peered above the rocks.

Garret was down in the little valley easily tying the men together. One appeared to be unconscious and the other was fighting a losing battle against Garret. Garret collected their weapons, then jogged back up the hill to her.

He returned, though still crouched behind the rocks, clearly knowing there could be more out there or coming toward the sound of the gunshot. "Okay, that's one vehicle, hopefully."

Betty checked her phone. "Granger got two separate pairs and Tucker and Elsie got one pair."

"How did Granger manage to take down four different guys already?" Garret grumbled. "Okay, that means at the least we have two guys still out there, but only if they were each alone in their vehicles."

"That's unlikely, isn't it?" Betty asked, though she already knew the answer. "If the rest are traveling in pairs."

"Very." Garret squinted out over the horizon again and then sighed. He pointed and Betty let her gaze follow in the same direction, squinting to make out what Garret was frowning at.

Then she let out one sharp curse.

## Chapter Twenty-Four

The men were far enough away that the crowd of people was hard to fully make out, but at least four to seven men stood in a small clump off in the distance. They were looking for the source of the gunshots, no doubt.

For the most part, their backs were toward where Betty and Garret were, but Garret knew they'd figure it out eventually. The injured men might be kind of hidden behind a swell of land, but one would likely yell for help eventually.

It was clear this group of men was in tactical gear, planning something bigger than the smaller groups of men they'd already taken out had been.

"Holden, Gabriel and Mallory are on their way," Betty said.

"Who… Never mind." More people gave them a better chance no matter who they were, and he trusted Betty to know which people on her team were trustworthy. "We need to meet up. I think that's what this group has done. Can you tell everyone to come up to that outcropping?" He pointed to the other ridge of rocks, farther east. Hopefully that would keep this group confused as to their whereabouts.

Betty nodded and tapped into her phone.

Then they moved. Garret kept the pace slow, watching behind them to make sure the group of men hadn't caught a glimpse of them. The dogs were well behaved and followed a surprising array of orders.

Betty slipped once, but she caught herself and waved him on. They managed to make it to the second ridge of rocks without being spotted. They both sat, leaning against the rocks, breathing heavily as the dogs followed orders to lie and wait.

Garret glanced at Betty. She had that look on her face, a mix of hurt and worry that made his heart ache. He reached out and took her hand, giving it a squeeze. "We're making progress."

Betty nodded and squeezed his hand back. "I know. I just don't know why… She should have trusted us. To help. To fight with her. It's so hard to understand why she wouldn't. When she has so many trained operatives at her fingertips. So many people who owe her… everything."

Garret thought about how complicated *owe* could be. "Maybe she didn't want to be owed."

"Or she didn't think she deserved it," Betty said with a sad frown. "Regardless, when it's all over, she's getting a piece of my mind."

Garret managed a smile. "She'll deserve it."

Betty turned her head, staring at him as her expression melted into something else. "Thank you."

"For what?"

"This isn't your fight. It hasn't been, this whole time. It was Nate's. It was Savannah's. It's mine. You're just…"

"It just so happens I care or cared about everyone on that list. So there's no place else I'd be."

"You're a good guy, Garret."

"You're a pretty good woman, Bet."

She inhaled deeply, then pointed. "North Star signal."

He didn't see anything, but soon a man in black appeared.

The North Star agent made his way over carefully and slowly, keeping his eyes on the men in the distance. He crouched in front of them. Garret didn't recognize him, but he grinned at Betty.

"Not quite the circumstances I wanted to see you again, Betty."

"Holden, you never wanted to see me," she returned good-naturedly. She pointed at the man as she glanced at Garret. "Terrified of doctors."

"'Terrified' seems harsh." He held out his hand. "Holden Parker."

"Garret Averly," Garret replied, shaking the man's hand.

"So, what have we got?"

They explained the situation and then waited awhile longer, each member of their team slowly appearing and joining them in their little hiding spot. Snow had begun to fall, but they all ignored it.

When Granger finally arrived, with a split lip and slight limp, no one asked him about it. They got down to brass tacks.

"We want a split," Garret said when no one seemed eager to take the reins. "Half our team on this side. Half our team on the inside. So we send four people—"

"Just three. Once they get to Shay, she'll be the fourth person," Mallory pointed out.

"She's right," Granger said gruffly. "I'll take Wyatt and—"

"Me," Elsie interrupted. "I need to get in and look at the comm units. See what's been compromised so we know what they know, what they've been watching."

Granger scowled. "Elsie."

She shook her head. "I'm coming one way or another. Might as well let me be part of the team."

Garret could tell Granger wanted to argue, but he swallowed it down. "Holden, you'll be in command out here. No offense, Averly."

Holden nodded.

Garret didn't argue about not being in charge. Somehow he'd gotten wrapped up in something that had nothing to do with him. He could play subordinate.

Probably.

"You four out here disarm this group while my group gets inside. We can't use the comm units, so we're just going to have to do our best to follow the plan. Text if you can but if stuff hits the fan, follow your team leader."

There was a quiet round of assent. Granger looked over the rock outcropping. "Still there," he muttered. "They're clearly planning something, so this can go all wrong. Be careful. Be smart. If we have to just get Shay out and leave headquarters behind, we can."

Garret didn't miss the look the North Star members shared. Almost a questioning if they were going to follow Granger's orders, but eventually they all nodded.

"We'll move forward on the group," Holden said. "Give you guys a diversion to get inside."

Granger nodded once sharply. "We'll start moving in the opposite direction." He signaled his team to move out and they crouch-walked toward the west—in the opposite direction to the group of men.

Holden studied Garret, Gabriel and Mallory. "We'll surround them. North, east, south, west. Betty, you're going to be our sniper backup and stay right here."

"I can't shoot, Holden. Ask Garret."

"No offense but you can't fight, either. We need someone to watch in case stuff goes wrong."

Betty scowled, but Garret put his hand on her arm. "He's right. We need someone who can call for extra backup, or who can stitch up any wounds. You can also warn us if something happens."

"We can't use the comm units."

"Can you whistle?"

"Well, sure."

"There you go. Long whistle for incoming danger. Short whistle telling us to get out."

Holden nodded. "Good idea. They might hear it, but it'll give us a chance to deal. If you do have to whistle, make sure you run after. Far away. We'll handle it. We don't want them going after you."

Betty pursed her lips. She didn't argue, but Garret hoped it wouldn't come to that, because he knew Betty wouldn't just run away. She'd stand there and fight.

He blew out an uneasy breath. He'd have to *make sure* it didn't come to that.

"All right. That's the plan. On the count of three?"

Everyone nodded, and Holden started counting off.

Garret leaned in and gave Betty a hard kiss. "Be safe," he said in a rough whisper.

She smiled at him. "You, too."

He nodded, then moved quietly and carefully toward the group of men. He pushed thoughts of his kids and Betty out of his mind and focused on what had to be done.

BETTY HATED STAYING back watching, but there was really no other recourse. She *couldn't* fight. She was a terrible shot. She'd joined North Star to *help*, not fight.

So she could only hide behind this rocky outcropping and watch. It reminded her far too much of her childhood. Of her father telling her to run far away before he walked into what he knew would be his end.

She'd become a doctor to make him proud. To do what he hadn't had the opportunity to do—actual good, not work for a gang. She'd never learned to fight because it felt like falling into what he'd given his life for her to escape.

Now she wished she'd learned. Turned herself into a machine like Shay or Sabrina had. But wishes didn't mean much in the midst of watching people she loved moving toward the group of armed men.

The dogs whined next to her, so she petted their heads. It calmed and steadied her. She had a function here. Maybe it wasn't in the thick of things, but it still mattered.

The group began to turn as her team approached. There was a gunshot, and one of the strangers went down. Her team attacked before anyone else could get a gunshot off. Their immediate goal to get rid of the guns, clearly.

She could see now there were six of the other men. From her vantage point, it was hard to parse what was happening, but they seemed to be fighting man-to-man.

Mallory took hers down first. Gabriel was next. They dragged their men out of the fray and tied them up. Then they joined Holden in the knock-down, drag-out with a large man who did not seem to want to go down.

Garret was struggling with his man, too. Likely because of his injured shoulder. Still, the man wasn't getting a chance to go to his gun. Betty looked back over at Holden. The man they were battling was debilitated, but Gabriel was lying in the snow, with Holden clearly patching up some injury he'd sustained. Mallory was struggling to tie all their quarry together.

Betty looked back at Garret. Still fighting, still keeping the man he was fighting from his gun, but that meant Garret didn't have his gun or couldn't get to his, either. So they fought, punching and kicking in the quickly falling snow.

Another new person approached a ways off from the group, not one of their own. Holden was still working on Gabriel, Mallory was still fighting with binding all of the group who'd been bested, Garret was still grappling with a man on the ground, and everyone was unaware.

Betty tried to whistle, but it must have been lost in the wind. The new man had a gun and was creeping up on the group.

He'd shoot Garret. Betty knew that.

And her whistle didn't seem to have been heard.

She sucked in a breath and stood. It was her moment.

To do what her father had once done for her. To do what Garret would have done for…anyone. Time and time again. It was who he was, what he'd dedicated his life to.

He said he'd sacrifice if there was no other choice, and she saw no other. So she acted.

She ordered the dogs to stay, and she started to run. She could shoot at the man. Even though her aim was terrible, the shot would scare him, take his attention away from Garret.

So she ran, and she shot. No matter how bad a shot it was, it was *something*.

The jarring jerk of the gun while she was running was unexpected, so she tripped a little bit. A return shot echoed through the air and Betty landed onto the snowy, frozen ground *hard*.

Her body rattled and she lost her grip on the gun. The fall knocked the wind out of her. She struggled to suck in a breath. Had she been shot? But she didn't feel—

"Betty. Betty."

Garret's voice, and suddenly he was next to her. He was touching her all over, rolling her this way and that in the snow. She was breathless, trying to make sense of what had happened as Garret searched her for some kind of wound.

But she'd only had the wind knocked out of her. Hit her head a little too hard.

"It didn't… It didn't hit me," she finally managed. "Nothing hit me."

They both looked to where the gunman lay in a heap. Just a little way beyond, Shay stood. Gun pointed at his still body.

Everyone else came running, guns at the ready. They

surveyed the area, then Granger started barking out orders. Everyone jumped to follow them.

Everyone except Shay. She kept standing there. Something was wrong. She was too pale. She held herself too…strangely.

Betty got to her feet and moved toward her as North Star operatives moved to clear out the men and call the necessary authorities. There was so much to do and still Shay didn't move. She stood there, gun still pointed—though the shot man had been moved.

"Shay?"

Shay's eyes were dull as she moved them to meet Betty's gaze. "Get inside, Bet. It's cold out."

Betty frowned through the snow. It was, but… That's when she noticed the pool of red, ever growing, underneath where Shay stood.

Betty swore and managed to grab Shay right before she swayed into unconsciousness.

## Chapter Twenty-Five

A few hours later, Garret sat in a meeting room inside North Star headquarters with the rest of the operatives, including Holden, who was apparently only a semi-retired operative, and Granger, who'd fallen back into his role as leader quite easily, in Garret's estimation.

Betty wasn't in the room. She was watching over Shay, who'd apparently taken a bullet to the gut inside headquarters before she'd made the shot that had saved Garret's life.

But it was over now. The members of the Vianni family hadn't expected an attack from the *outside*. They'd been prepared to blow up headquarters, Shay included.

At least, that was the story. If they'd been planning on blowing up the place, why had someone gotten inside and shot Shay?

Garret didn't ask that question, though. He figured that was North Star's deal. He, personally, was ready to get his babies and head home and forget everything about North Star.

Well, not everything.

"The Feds have been closing in on the Viannis

the past few months because of their connection to the groups you guys have been taking care of—the Lorens and Ross Industries and so on. Which is why they got desperate enough to come here. They'd lost their military weapons supplier when you took down Loren. They didn't like that North Star had stopped them at every turn, again, so it was…personal, in a way."

"That doesn't explain how they knew we were *here*," Mallory pointed out. "Who we are. Where our head-quarters is."

"That's where Savannah comes in," Elsie said. "She was connected to her grandfather, obviously, but along with Courtney they managed to grab one of our comm units when Garret was shot back in Montana. Savan-nah got it to Cliff, who was the Viannis' tech person. He hacked his way into our system—not just to listen to us, but to use GPS coordinates to find our head-quarters."

"So we took down Cliff. Then they send in the Viannis to take down us. But that doesn't explain Shay," Daniels said.

"She sent us all away to handle it herself," Mallory said, her voice flat.

Gabriel, who'd been grazed by a bullet during the whole scuffle, sat next to Mallory looking angry. "And got herself shot in the process."

Granger stood in front of the group, looking grave. "Betty says she'll make it."

"Yeah, but why'd she do it?" Elsie asked, looking hurt and confused. "Why would she send everyone away when she had an entire team at her disposal? It doesn't make any sense."

It didn't. Not to Garret, and clearly not to anyone else in the room.

Except maybe Granger.

BETTY SAT NEXT to Shay's bed, holding her hand while she slept. A drug-induced sleep, but sleep nonetheless. It'd wear off soon enough, and then recovery would begin. The gunshot had been nasty, the blood loss worse. Betty had worked on her, and then Mara had arrived to assist.

Shay would make it, but recovery would be difficult. Especially if Shay herself was difficult.

Shay's eyes blinked open. Slowly, she came to consciousness, the clouds in her eyes clearing. She sighed heavily. "Well, gonna live, huh?"

"What were you thinking?" Betty demanded, though she knew she should give Shay time. But she…couldn't. "To send us all away. To handle this on your own."

Shay shifted uncomfortably in the bed, but Betty didn't let her hand go. And Shay didn't let go or try to pull away, either.

"I was thinking that you all didn't have a thing to do with my past."

Betty frowned at that. It wasn't what Granger had explained to her. So she decided to start there. "What about Granger?" Betty demanded.

Shay shifted again, frowning as she tried to pull her hand away from Betty. But Betty held firm. "We might have been connected, but same goes. He wasn't…"

"They were after North Star. Because of the weapons stuff. Not you. Granger said so. Why would you think it's personal?"

Shay let out a long breath. "Maybe it was coincidence. But...I was part of that family once, Bet. I *was* a Vianni. I knew what they were capable of. I couldn't risk you all."

"You'd be dead if we hadn't risked ourselves."

"Yeah."

"You *knew* you'd wind up dead."

"I had a plan."

But she didn't elaborate and suddenly Betty was too tired to press. "You need rest. You need to follow doctor's orders, but I am so angry with you."

"I know. Keep in mind, I saved your guy's life."

"Guilt trip. Impressive. Maybe you'll be okay after all."

"Maybe," Shay agreed. "This can't change your plans. I don't need you to stay. You're a fantastic doctor. Half of us would be dead if we hadn't had you."

"Including you, a few different times."

"Including me a few different times." Shay smiled a little. "But you weren't made for this. Your dad sacrificed to get you away from the Sons and on to something better than what he had."

"Working for North Star is far better than working for the Sons."

"Maybe, but you know what you'd be really good at?"

"What?"

"A little clinic in a small town in Montana, shacked up with this hot cop and his two kids."

God, the idea of it made her chest ache. It was what

she wanted. That real future so many of her friends had built. But not Shay. She wanted that for Shay, but she had to accept that maybe Shay didn't want it for herself. "Don't forget the dog."

Shay laughed, then winced.

"I'm not leaving this place until I'm sure you're on the mend."

"What will your cop have to say about that?"

Betty considered. "He'll understand. He understands loyalty, Shay. I wish you did."

"Bet." She sighed. "You're the best friend I've got. I love you. I couldn't have stood it if you or anyone I love had gotten caught in this cross fire. Maybe you guys can't ever forgive me for that, but it was the only choice I could live with. Even if you guys ruined it."

Betty thought about what Garret had said. How it wasn't so much about sacrifice as what you could live with. How could she blame Shay for what she could live with?

She smoothed some hair off Shay's forehead. "I love you, too. Rest now. We'll figure everything else out once you're better."

Betty's heart still hurt that Shay would have chosen going it alone over help, but she supposed they'd come to a kind of understanding. It was a turning point, for both of them. Betty couldn't predict how Shay's life would turn out, but Shay was right.

Hers was going to be a little clinic in Montana with a hot cop and two adorable kids. And a dog.

# *Epilogue*

Garret had gone back to Blue Valley with his babies alone. He'd introduced his parents to their grandchildren and his brother to his niece and nephew. His shoulder was mostly healed. With the help of his mother baby-sitting, he'd gone back to work. Back to his normal life.

It felt empty without Betty by his side. They talked every night on the phone, and Shay was getting closer to being back on her feet, so Betty would make the move to Blue Valley soon. They'd agreed on that.

So the time gave him a chance to plan. Prepare. He'd found a couple buildings he thought she could lease to start her own clinic, not far from his police station. Not that anything in Blue Valley was far, but he liked the idea of being close. He liked the idea of her *here*.

A knock sounded on the door and Garret abandoned the sad box mac and cheese he'd been starting to prepare for a late dinner to answer it. When he opened the door, Betty stood there on his stoop, snow falling around her.

"Hi," she offered, her eyes bright, her smile wide.

"You're…back."

A raucous bark came from deep in the house and

then the clatter of nails on the hardwood as Barney came racing. He jumped at Betty before Garret could stop him. Garret did manage to grab Betty so Barney didn't knock her off the stoop.

But she laughed and crouched and scratched Barney's ears. "Oh, I missed your face." She laughed again as Barney licked her and whined and turned in circles of excitement.

"All right," Garret grumbled. "Let her inside, you oaf."

He managed to pull Barney off Betty and then get them both inside. It felt…strange for a moment, to have her back. To feel like the past few weeks hadn't happened and they were back to doctor and patient.

She shrugged out of her coat, not quite meeting his gaze. "I was going to wait a few more days, but Shay practically shoved me into Granger's plane."

Garret had had a plan, but it went out the window. He pulled her into his arms, lifted her off her feet and pressed his mouth to hers. She laughed into the kiss, wrapping her arms around his neck.

"Don't tell me they're asleep."

"We'll go look in on them. Maybe Barney woke them up."

He pulled her back to their room that his mother had decorated. In the glow of the night-light, they were both fast asleep.

Betty sighed. "They've grown a foot," she whispered. There were tears in her eyes, but she blinked them away. She pulled him back out of the room.

"We can wake them—"

"No. Never wake a sleeping baby. There will be plenty of time to love on them."

"They took your room."

Betty's expression shuttered. "Oh, well. It's their room. I was only a…guest."

Garret reached out and brushed a piece of hair off her face. "What are you now?"

She looked up at him. "What do you want me to be?"

He held up a hand. "Stay right there."

He went back into his room. Nerves fluttered, indecision threatened, but he knew. He *knew*. And he'd made enough mistakes in his life to know that trying to avoid them, trying to get the timing right, didn't stop the mistakes. Nothing did.

He'd rather be with someone who'd forgive the mistakes than worry about making them. He returned and she was curled up on his couch, Barney practically in her lap, though he was way too big.

She smiled up at him and, yeah, he didn't have any doubts. No indecision. No matter what she had to say about it, this was what he wanted. So he'd put it on the line, and hopefully it was what she wanted, too.

"I had this all planned out. I was going to show you the building for rent you could start your clinic in. Talk up the town. Use the babies and Barney to soften you up."

"Soften me up for what?"

He held the ring out. Betty gaped at it.

"If it's too fast, I can put it away until it's not."

"No," she said, breathlessly. "Sometimes… Sometimes you grab what's good, fast or slow. Because it's right. This is right."

She let him slide the ring onto her finger. She looked at it, then laughed, a few tears slipping onto her cheeks. It was the first time he'd seen her cry, though she'd been close through everything they'd gone through.

But it was happiness that finally made her cry, and there was something good about that. She wiped the tears away. "Are you… You have the ring—you're sure. You're sure and I'm sure." She took a deep breath, looking up from the ring to him. "I'm sure," she whispered.

He pulled her to him. Small and soft in his embrace. The perfect fit here. Even with Barney trying to wiggle between them. "I'm glad you're home, Bet."

"Yeah, home." She let out a long sigh, leaning her head on his shoulder. "Me, too."

\* \* \* \* \*

# WE HOPE YOU ENJOYED
## THIS BOOK FROM

**HARLEQUIN**

# INTRIGUE

*Seek thrills. Solve crimes. Justice served.*

Dive into action-packed stories that will keep you
on the edge of your seat. Solve the crime
and deliver justice at all costs.

**6 NEW BOOKS AVAILABLE EVERY MONTH!**

COMING NEXT MONTH FROM

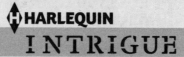

# INTRIGUE

## #2073 STICKING TO HER GUNS
*A Colt Brothers Investigation* • by B.J. Daniels

Tommy Colt is stunned when his childhood best friend—and love—
Bella Worthington abruptly announces she's engaged to their old-time nemesis!
Knowing her better than anyone, Tommy's convinced something is dangerously
wrong. Now Colt Brothers Investigations' newest partner is racing to uncover the
truth and ask Bella a certain question...if they survive.

## #2074 FOOTHILLS FIELD SEARCH
*K-9s on Patrol* • by Maggie Wells

When two kids are kidnapped from plain sight, Officer Brady Nichols and his
intrepid canine, Winnie, spring into action. Single mother Cassie Whitaker thought
she'd left big-city peril behind—until it followed her to Jasper. But can Brady and
his K-9 protect Cassie from a stalker who won't take no for an answer?

## #2075 NEWLYWED ASSIGNMENT
*A Ree and Quint Novel* • by Barb Han

Hardheaded ATF legend Quint Casey knows he's playing with fire asking
Agent Ree Sheppard to re-up as his undercover wife. To crack a ruthless Houston
weapons ring, they must keep the mission—and their explosive chemistry—under
control. But Quint's determined need for revenge and Ree's risky moves are
putting everything on the line...

## #2076 UNDERCOVER RESCUE
*A North Star Novel Series* • by Nicole Helm

After the husband she thought was dead returns with revenge on his mind,
Veronica Shay resolves to confront her secret past—and her old boss,
Granger Macmillan, won't let her handle it on her own. But when they fall into a
nefarious trap, they'll call in their entire North Star family in order to stay alive...

## #2077 COLD CASE CAPTIVE
*The Saving Kelby Creek Series* • by Tyler Anne Snell

Returning to Kelby Creek only intensifies Detective Lily Howard's guilt at the
choice she made years ago to rescue her childhood crush, Anthony Perez, rather
than pursue the man abducting his sister. But another teen girl's disappearance
offers a chance to work with Ant again—and a tantalizing new lead that could
mean inescapable danger.

## #2078 THE HEART-SHAPED MURDERS
*A West Coast Crime Story* • by Denise N. Wheatley

Attacked and left with a partial heart-shaped symbol carved into her chest,
forensic investigator Lena Love finds leaving LA to return to her hometown comes
with its own danger—like detective David Hudson, the love she left behind.
But soon bodies—all marked with the killer's signature heart—are discovered in
David's jurisdiction...

**YOU CAN FIND MORE INFORMATION ON UPCOMING HARLEQUIN TITLES,
FREE EXCERPTS AND MORE AT HARLEQUIN.COM.**

HICNM0422

*Wedding bells and shotgun fire are ringing out
in Lonesome, Montana. Read on for another
Colt Brothers Investigation novel from* New York Times
*bestselling author B.J. Daniels.*

Bella Worthington took a breath and, opening her eyes, finally faced her reflection in the full-length mirror. The wedding dress fit perfectly—just as he'd said it would. While accentuating her curves, the neckline was modest, the drape flattering. As much as she hated to admit it, Fitz had good taste.

The sapphire-and-diamond necklace he'd given her last night gleamed at her throat, bringing out the blue-green of her eyes—also like he'd said it would. He'd thought of everything—right down to the huge pear-shaped diamond engagement ring on her finger. All of it would be sold off before the ink dried on the marriage license—if she let it go that far.

As she studied her reflection, though, she realized this was exactly as he'd planned it. She looked the beautiful bride on her wedding day. No one would be the wiser.

She could hear music and the murmur of voices downstairs. He'd invited the whole town of Lonesome, Montana. She'd watched from the upstairs window as the guests had arrived earlier. He'd wanted an audience for this and now he would have one.

The knock at the door startled her, even though she'd been expecting it. "It's time," said a male voice on the other side. One of Fitz's hired bodyguards, Ronan, was waiting. He would be carrying a weapon under his suit. Security, she'd been told, to keep her safe. A lie.

She listened as Ronan unlocked her door and waited outside, his boss not taking any chances. He had made sure there was no possibility of escape short of shackling her to her bed. Fitz was determined that she find no way out of this. It didn't appear that she had.

In a few moments, she would be escorted downstairs to where her maid of honor and bridesmaids were waiting—all handpicked by her groom. If they'd questioned why they were down there and she was up here, they hadn't asked. He wasn't the kind of man women questioned. At least not more than once.

For another moment, Bella stared at the stranger in the mirror. She didn't have to wonder how she'd gotten to this point in her life. Unfortunately, she knew too well. She'd just never thought Fitz would go this far. Her mistake. He, however, had no idea how far she was willing to go to make sure the wedding never happened.

Taking a breath, she picked up her bouquet from her favorite local flower shop. The bouquet had been a special order delivered earlier. Her hand barely trembled as she lifted the blossoms to her nose for a moment, taking in the sweet scent of the tiny white roses—also his choice. Carefully, she separated the tiny buds, afraid it wouldn't be there.

It took her a few moments to find the long, slim silver blade hidden among the roses and stems. The blade was sharp, and lethal if used correctly. She knew exactly how to use it. She slid it back into the bouquet out of sight. He wouldn't think to check it. She hoped. He'd anticipated her every move and attacked with one of his own. Did she really think he wouldn't be ready for anything?

Making sure the door was still closed, she checked her garter. What she'd tucked under it was still there, safe, at least for the moment.

Another knock at the door. Fitz would be getting impatient and no one wanted that. "Everyone's waiting," Ronan said, tension in his tone. If this didn't go as meticulously planned, there would be hell to pay from his boss. Something else they all knew.

She stepped to the door and opened it, lifting her chin and straightening her spine. Ronan's eyes swept over her with a lusty gaze, but he stepped back as if not all that sure of her. Clearly he'd been warned to be wary of her. Probably just as she'd been warned what would happen if she refused to come down—or worse, made a scene in front of the guests.

At the bottom of the stairs, the room opened and she saw Fitz waiting for her with the person he'd hired to officiate.

He was so confident that he'd backed her into a corner with no way out. He'd always underestimated her. Today would be no different. But he didn't know her as well as he thought. He'd held her prisoner, threatened her, forced her into this dress and this ruse.

But that didn't mean she was going to marry him.

She would kill him first.

*Don't miss*
**Sticking to Her Guns** *by B.J. Daniels,*
*available June 2022 wherever*
*Harlequin books and ebooks are sold.*

Harlequin.com

HIEXP0322INC

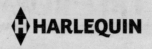

# HARLEQUIN

*Heartfelt or thrilling, passionate or uplifting—Harlequin is more than just happily-ever-after.*

With twelve different series to choose from and new books available every month, you are sure to find stories that will move you, uplift you, inspire and delight you.

SIGN UP FOR THE
...SLETTER

...t great new
...offers!

...ewsletters